I0699672

PRINCES

A novella by

Noah Khan

This story is dedicated to my family.
Thank you for always encouraging me to follow
my dreams!

PROLOGUE

a long time ago, in the distant past...

I moved as quickly as I could, trying not to make a sound. I held my breath and opened the door to my chambers as quietly as possible, praying to the gods that it doesn't creak. Once I was able to exit my chambers, I made my way across the grandiose hallway and down the carved white marble staircase. My white silk cape dragged across the wooden floor and I pulled the hood over my head tightly. After what seemed like forever, I reached the front doors, emblazoned with our family crest into the fine wood. I hesitated; I turned around and I realized this may be the last time I ever set foot in this castle. I thought to myself, *am I making the right choice?* Then I thought of his face and his clear blue eyes. And I thought of his smile. And the freckles scattered across his pale nose. Then I was sure, right then, that I was making the right decision. I opened the doors and the cold night air greeted me like an old friend, like it was waiting for me.

I was glad I wore my white silk robes with my hood because it was bitter cold out. I walked toward the stables and I could hear my heart pumping in my chest. I greeted the horses and went to my favorite horse at the end. Her fur is a dark brown and her name is Princess Lola. Okay, she's not really a princess but in my mind she has her own kingdom. She is beloved by her people and is a great ruler. I saddled her up and then I jumped on her back, stroking her mane.

My throat was dry as I whispered to her, "Are you ready?" She didn't answer, but I knew what she was thinking: that I am the one who isn't ready. But I'd made it this far and I knew I could not turn back now. I snapped the reins and we were off, galloping down the dirt path, my cloak flying behind me in the wind. We rode like this for quite some time, the cool night air hitting my face. Until finally, I saw familiar shapes beginning to form and the castle of Dynalis coming closer. The castle is huge-even bigger than our own castle, and is built in a rococo-style, very extravagant with lots of gold. As I drew closer to the castle, I commanded Lola to stop and I dismounted. I tied her to a nearby tree and I stroked her mane. I knew this part would be coming, but I was not ready. Tears welled in my eyes and I hugged her. I knew that this was probably the last time I'd ever see her. She seemed to know this too because she made a little wail.

"Goodbye, my sweet princess," I whispered. I knew someone from the castle would find her and take her in as their own, as horses are hard to come by in these parts. I stroked her head one last time before I turned around, pulled my hood up and walked down the path toward the castle. It was now or never.

And then I saw him. He was waiting for me, and my heart raced, like it always does when I see him again. He emerged from behind a pillar by the entrance of the castle and smiled at me. He extended his hand and I took it.

"Come," he said. "We must hurry. We don't have much time." We ran together, hand in hand to behind the castle, where there is an underground cellar used for shelter from intense tornadoes or hurricanes. We climbed down the steps into the ground. It was dark, but Alec turned on a light and I saw there were supplies and boxes containing food. "I believe this should be sufficient for our travels," he said. I looked at the boxes. I didn't say anything. He stared at me, then came closer and stroked my cheek. "Hey," he said. "Are you alright?"

I tried to nod but I couldn't. Doubt clouded my mind. "Are we doing the right thing?" I asked. "I know we said that we would run away so we can be together, but…"

Alec stared at me, compassion in his eyes. "Having second thoughts?" he asked.

I shook my head. "No. I want to be with you, I do. But I also feel bad abandoning my people."

Alec sighed. "I understand how you feel. I feel the same. But if we don't do this, there is no other way for us to be together. You understand that, right?" I understood this. And it killed me inside. I knew that my father would be horrified to learn that his only son was a sodomite and sleeping with the enemy. I know what needs to be done. I opened my mouth to say that I'm ready, then the world exploded.

I heard what sounded like a bomb exploding. Alec and I went silent and our eyes widened. He lifted a finger to his mouth for me to stay silent and unsheathed his sword.

"I'll go see what that was," he whispered and I nodded, but really I wanted to beg him to stay with me because I was terrified. I watched him run up the stairs and he lifted the door to the cellar and climbed out. A couple of seconds passed, and that is when I heard the screaming.

I ran up the cellar stairs and burst from the ground. At first, I couldn't make out anything. There was smoke everywhere and I had to cover my mouth because all I smelled was smoke and something burning. I looked around as my vision cleared up and I, too, began to scream when I saw the bodies on the ground. I know now that what was burning was human flesh. I ran around aimlessly, looking for Alec but I didn't see him anywhere. I could vaguely see the guards run out of the castle with their swords swinging at something. A figure emerged from the smoke and fire, and my heart froze: Father.

But no. That can't be father. His eyes were blood red and there was blood spilling from his mouth like foam. He was tall, much taller than I remember and he was…smiling. He lifted a hand up and all of the guards were swallowed by flames. I covered my mouth in horror just as Alec jumped in front of me with his sword. My father walked toward us.

"Don't come any closer!" Alec yelled.

My father tilted his head. "So…you are the one who has sullied and defiled my son?" he asked, blood spurting out like spit. I didn't even recognize his voice. It sounded deep, monstrous, and demonic. "I have something special in store for you." Suddenly Alec was thrust up into the air like a rag doll, sword dropped to the floor. I screamed.

"Damien, get out of here!" Alec screamed.

Tears streamed down my face as I finally made eye contact with this thing that had become my father. His smile dropped and he stared at me hungrily. "You," is all he said. Then Alec's beautiful pale face became contorted and I saw his backbone begin to snap backward.

"NOOOO!" I screamed. I picked up the sword and lunged toward my father, but he held out his hand and threw me against a tree, knocking the wind out of me. I came to, and I looked at Alec with his broken bones in the air and he looked at me.

"I love you." He smiled sadly. And then he erupted into flames.

I screamed, "What have you done?! You sick bastard!" I ran toward this evil creature and suddenly I was thrown into the air. What was once my father now looked at me.

"You are the sick one, child, sleeping with the enemy and allowing yourself to be defiled by filth. I shall be the ruler of this world and eliminate all of the filth!" Then he smiled. "Starting with my own kin." Then I felt flames begin to lick my legs and make their way up to my torso.

I shut my eyes in pain and I screamed. *No. I can't allow this to happen. Not yet.* I thought about the life I'd lived. I thought about my mother and I thought about Lola. I thought about my father, and even though he was cruel, I still loved him. And then I thought about Alec and his sweet freckles. And I thought about the way he first kissed me. My hands felt hot, but it wasn't the flames this time. I felt a power surging within me, desperate to get out. I opened my eyes, screamed, and thrusted out my hands, a bright light erupting from them that made contact with my father's torso. His smile faded as he disintegrated into ash. He screamed in pain, then we were both screaming. A black shadow ejected itself from my father and shot into the night sky. When the flames finally engulfed me fully, my last thought was, *Please, God, let me have a happy life.*

CHAPTER 1

Present Day, New York

Damien

Beep, beep, beep…
Beep, beep, beep.

I turned in my bed and groaned. Why does morning have to come so quickly? I sighed and hit the snooze button on my phone. Then I turned over and closed my eyes again, trying to go back to the dream I was having. I can't recall what it was about exactly, but I do remember a hot guy being in it. Suddenly, a pillow hit my face and my roommate Karina yelled, "Damien, it's eight! You're gonna be late for class. Again." I sighed and sat up groggily, rubbing my eyes. Karina sat on the opposite side of the room doing her makeup.

I looked at her with my crusty eyes and said, "I'm tired. I don't wanna go."

Karina laughed. "You're like a child," she said.

I reluctantly got up to take a shower. As I undressed, I turned the water on. I stood there in the shower, closing my eyes and letting the warm water run down my body. I thought about my dream and the hot guy in it. I sighed and thought about how nice it would be to have a boyfriend. Alas, we don't always get what we want. After my shower, I got out and assessed my clothing options. I decided on a pair of clean dark jeans and a yellow buttercream cardigan. I put on my signature seahorse pendant that once belonged to my mother. I checked my reflection in the mirror.

"How do I look?" I asked.

Karina gave me a once-over. "Gay."

I laughed and threw a pillow at her. I should've known that's what she'd say. Karina asked if I was finally ready. I nodded and grabbed my phone and backpack and we headed out.

The walk to campus isn't too far from our dorm. Karina and I passed by the busy streets of New York and I smiled, still not believing that I was actually attending this school. It'd been a dream of mine since I was little to attend NYU and become an actor. I know, I know, it's a cliche for the gays, but it's still my dream. We passed by a hot dog truck when Karina said, "So. Any guys?"

I gave her the side-eye and sighed. "I think you know the answer to that question."

Karina pouted, her blond hair moving in the wind. "Still nothing? Not even on the apps?"

I laughed bitterly, "The apps suck. Either you get ghosted mid-conversation, or you don't get a reply at all."

Karina groaned. "Damn, that sucks."

I nodded. It really did suck. I thought a plus of going to school would be meeting a cute guy and getting a boyfriend, but I guess things don't always work out like that. Once we neared campus, Karina and I went our separate ways to class. Karina and I were both freshmen last year and we instantly clicked. We just have the same sense of humor and get along great. I'm glad to have made at least one friend in The Big Apple. Not that I don't have friends, I do. It's just that sometimes I feel like I have more acquaintances than friends. I don't know.

When I entered my acting class, I saw the familiar bright red hair of my teacher, Ms. Simmons. Instead of normal desks and chairs, the room was furnished with couches, beanbags, and other chairs that seemed to have been taken from *Alice In Wonderland*. I sat on a couch and Ms. Simmons rose up from her desk and addressed us.

"So, I have an announcement for you all. We have a new student joining us today." I'm taken aback. Everyone in the class murmurs and looks around, shocked because it's the middle of the year—an odd time for transfer students.

"Quiet down," Ms. Simmons said. "Please, welcome Alec Caldwell".

My mouth literally dropped open. In walked one of the *hottest* guys I have ever seen. He had dark black hair, almost a blue-black, with sideswept bangs. He wore a bomber jacket and black Vans. And when I got a closer look, I saw he had crystal blue eyes with a scattering of freckles across his pale face. The only thing is, he's not smiling. In fact, it almost looked like he was frowning at something. And then I realized he was looking *at me.* What the hell?

When Ms. Simmons told Alec he can sit wherever he'd like, it seemed like he chose to sit as far away from me as possible. What the hell was going on? I was so lost in thought that I didn't realize Ms. Simmons was pairing us up for an exercise. I prayed to whatever higher power exists that I didn't get paired up with this Alec guy because not only am I intimidated by his hotness, but it also seems like he hates me already.

"Alec," Ms. Simmons said, "You can go with Damien." And my insides flip inside out. *Of. Fucking. Course.* Obviously whatever higher power I prayed to just gave me the middle finger. I looked at Alec and he looked at me with a glare.

"I'd like to pair up with someone else," he said.

The class went silent. I had to restrain myself from gasping. Did he actually just say that? Ms. Simmons looked taken aback as the rest of us. Then she composed herself.

"Alec, I'm aware you are new here but you will abide by my rules as long as you're in my class. This isn't high school. Go sit next to Damien."

I had to pinch myself to stop from screaming and dying of embarrassment. Alec sighed and made his way toward me. My heartbeat quickened. Even though he was an ass, he was still super-hot. He sat next to me without even looking at me or greeting me. I wondered if I smelled bad or something. I put deodorant on this morning, I remember that for a fact.

Ms. Simmons explained that we were going to do a two-person scene from any play we'd like, and that it can be dramatic or comedic. After the instructions, everyone went to their own spaces to choose a scene. My skin felt like it was on fire, and I looked at Alec. God, even his side profile was attractive. Alec could feel my eyes on him and looked back at me.

"Is there a problem?" he asked.

I quickly looked away. "No, there's no problem. But, um, I think we should probably start looking for a scene to do."

Alec rolled his blue eyes and scoffed. "Listen. I'm only in this class because I needed extra credits. I have no interest in performing anything, especially with you."

My skin scorched and my blood began to boil. I like to think of myself as a kindhearted person, but I couldn't do it anymore.

I turned to him and before I could stop myself I said, "Why are you acting like such an asshole? You don't even know me and yet you're acting like I'm your worst enemy. Did I do something to offend you?"

Alec stared at me and stayed silent. He stared at me for so long I began to get uncomfortable.

He looked away finally and said, "Fine, Damien. I'll work on this scene with you. You can choose, I don't care what we do."

I opened my mouth to say something, but then class was over. Alec jumped up with his long legs and left without saying goodbye, of course, or even giving me his phone number so we could talk about our scene. I sighed. Of course out of all the people in this class I get paired up with a jerk.

At least he's easy on the eyes.

Karina burst out laughing in Starbucks when I told her what happened in class that day. I glared at her. "It's not funny!" I exclaimed.

Karina was still laughing as she tied her long blond hair into a topknot.

"He literally wanted a different partner?" she asked.

I nodded. "Literally."

She shook her head and took a sip from her latte. "That is hilarious. But you said he was hot?"

I nodded. "Yeah, even though I hate to admit it, he's like the most attractive guy I've ever seen. Like ever." I took a sip from my pink Frappuccino. "He has these…intense blue eyes that suck you in and these freckles that scatter across his pale nose. And he has this jet black hair with long bangs and even though he was wearing a jacket, you could tell he was pretty built."

Karina stared at me with her mouth dropped open, mid-sip from her latte. I frowned. "What?" I asked.

"Oh my god. You like this jerk."

Now *my* mouth dropped open. "What?! I absolutely do not like him! He-he's an asshole!" I slammed my Frappuccino down and said, "Yeah, he may be hot but that doesn't mean I *like* him!"

Karina shook her head. "I dunno. You got this look in your eye when you were describing him."

I gave her a mean look. "You're imagining things."

Karina shrugged. "I don't know. Maybe you two were lovers or something in a past life."

I burst out laughing. "Get these weird ideas out of your head."

Karina laughed too. "What? You never know!" I rolled my eyes and Karina looked at her phone. "Ugh, I gotta go to my next class. But I'll see you at our dorm later, yeah?"

I nodded as she gathered her things and waved good-bye. I started to gather my backpack and books when I felt eyes on me. When I turned around to see, there was no one there besides the other customers sitting at tables and talking. I turned back and sighed. Maybe *I'm* the one who is going crazy. I walked toward the exit and thought about what Karina said and I laughed to myself. *Past lovers.*

Yeah, right.

A long time ago
The First Meeting

I knew I shouldn't be here. I knew that. But I couldn't help myself. I was just so curious to see what the Prince of Dynalis looked like. I heard rumors but had never seen him myself. I heard that he was handsome and strong. I heard that he has the bluest eyes you can imagine. I wanted to see what he looked like, just once. Just to satiate my curiosity. *And then I won't ever sneak out of the castle again,* I told myself. I could see men guarding the entrance to the castle but I heard that the prince often liked to tend to the gardens behind the castle. I was hoping he was there and I could catch a glimpse of him.

I quietly walked the dirt path around the giant castle and hid behind one of the giant trees. I gasped because the gardens were so much more beautiful than I expected. There were huge marble pillars that lined the garden and a fountain in the middle spouting clear blue water from a sculpture of an angel. There was also an enormous wooden gazebo, and then my heart stopped. In that gazebo was a man with black hair. He was watering one of the plants. The man turned around to water another plant and I felt like I was frozen in time. Standing there was the most gorgeous man I had ever seen. I knew then that the rumors were true about his blue eyes. They really were the color of the Earth. And he has freckles scattered across his pale face. His tall frame was dressed in beautiful dark blue robes. I stepped forward onto a branch, which snapped. My heart dropped and I stopped breathing. The prince turned and looked around. He put the can down and stepped forward, unsheathing a large sword that was hidden on his belt.

"Who's there?" he yelled. And wow. He had an alluring deep voice, a voice fitting of a man that will be king one day. I realized that I was caught and I gingerly stepped out from behind the tree. The prince and I made eye contact. For a few seconds, there was silence and again I felt as though time had frozen. The dream was ruined when he pointed his sword at my throat.

"Who are you, trespasser, and what do you want?" My eyes widened and my heart leapt to my throat, and I was unable to speak. I tried to think of a lie, of a reason why I'd be here. Then I realized he doesn't know who I am. That I was the Prince of Krusada, the enemy kingdom.

Finally able to get some words out, I said, "I…I came to see you." And then I wanted to slap myself because I was supposed to lie. The prince frowned.

"Why?" he asked. I stared at him, the blade still at my throat.

"I…I suppose I wanted to see if the rumors were true."

"What rumors?" The prince tilted his head.

"If your eyes are really as blue as they say." I smiled. And was beyond myself—I've never been so bold before. The prince stared at me for a couple more seconds, then lowered his sword.

"Well. I see. And are they?" I blushed and I nodded. "What's your name?" he asked.

"D…" I started, then I realized that now I do need to lie for real. "Dimitri," I said. The prince gave me a heart melting smile.

"My name is Alec. Prince Alec of Dynalis."

"I know." I smiled again.

He looked around. "What do you think of my garden?"

I admired the plants and flowers and pillars and fountains. "It's beautiful," I said—and I meant it. It really was beautiful and other-worldly. Just like Prince Alec.

"Would you like a tour of the castle? It's even more beautiful than my gardens," Alec said.

I laughed. "Why are you so trusting of me all of a sudden? I'm a trespasser after all."

Alec smiled. "Well, you don't seem like an immediate threat. And… I don't know. Something in my intuition tells me you mean no harm. And my intuition is usually right."

I smiled dumbly and opened my mouth to say that I would love a tour, but then I realized that I couldn't stay. I was due back home for my studies, and if I were gone too long the guards would be suspicious. "I can't. I actually have to go now," I said sadly and I began to walk back to Lola, who was tied to a nearby tree.

"Wait," Alec said. I turned around, grateful for another excuse to look at those eyes. "Will I see you again, trespasser?" he asked. I was silent for a moment because I didn't know. I told myself that I would never sneak out again. But then I looked back at Alec's hopeful expression and I couldn't bring myself to say no.

Instead, I smiled at him and I said, "I hope so. I really do."

CHAPTER 2

Present Day, New York

Damien

I was sitting on the couch in my dorm with Karina watching an episode of *Pretty Little Liars,* but I was too distracted to focus on the show. I kept on thinking of that new guy, and how infuriating he was. Where does he get off, acting like that? Who does he think he is? But then I kept thinking about his stupid blue eyes and freckles. Ugh, I'm disgusted with myself.

Karina turned to look at me. "Hey, are you good?"

"What do you mean?" I asked.

Karina gave me a look and paused the show. The look that says *stop bullshitting.* "You aren't even paying attention to the show and Hanna literally just got hit by a car."

I sighed. "It's…it's just I'm still angry about how I was treated by that new guy."

Karina laughed. "Oh my God. You're still hung up on that? He was an asshole, so what? Not everybody in this world is nice."

I looked away. "I know that. But…"

"But what?"

I stayed silent for a while. "You're gonna think I'm crazy, but I feel like I've met him before."

Karina tilted her head and frowned. "In what way?"

I shrugged. "I don't know. I feel like maybe I met him in a dream…or something like that."

Karina stared at me. Then she turned off the TV and got up. "It's getting late and I think you need some sleep."

I got up too. "I knew you were gonna think I'm crazy!"

Karina laid down on her bed and said, "I don't think you're crazy. But I do think you need some rest."

I walked to the bathroom to brush my teeth. "Fine, maybe you're right." About a minute later, I heard a noise. It sounded like…a bang or something coming from outside. I spit into the sink and returned to the room to ask Karina if she heard anything, but she was already asleep. Damn her ability to fall asleep in seconds. I hesitated for a moment, then decided to investigate. I grabbed my favorite red coat and quietly walked out our door, then downstairs to the main doors. Once outside, I looked around but I didn't see anything. I turned to go back inside, when out of the corner of my eye I saw a shadow move. My heart dropped and I sprinted back inside, up the stairs and into my room and locked the door. No way in hell was I investigating anymore. I wasn't trying to get killed. I went into the bathroom, my heart beating fast. What the hell *was that*? I mean, yeah, there were always sketchy people in New York's streets, but this was a relatively safe place. I got into bed and I tried to go to sleep, hoping that whatever that was went away.

Morning eventually came, but I was exhausted. After that experience, I could barely sleep. I looked at my phone. It was 8:15 a.m. Shit, I was gonna be late again. I looked at Karina's bed and saw that she already left. I sighed and got dressed because I didn't have time to take a shower. I shoved a piece of toast in my mouth, grabbed my backpack, and sprinted out the door.

I ran to my next class, which is my History of Theater and Film class, also taught by Ms. Simmons. When I arrived, Ms. Simmons was already in the middle of a lecture and she gave me a look—a look that said *late again, I see.* I blushed and quickly took my seat and grabbed my notebook. And then I froze. That *asshole* was also in this class. What the fuck? Was he stalking me or something? He was sitting at a desk toward the back, wearing a black hoodie, jeans, and the same black Vans. I scoffed to myself and planned to ignore him. I took down Ms. Simmons's notes and eventually the class was over.

Ms. Simmons cleared her throat. "Before you go, I want to announce that auditions for our musical are next week. The musical will be *Carrie*, based on the novel by Stephen King."

I almost screamed. *Carrie* is one of my favorite books ever. In fact, Carrie is a role I've always dreamed of playing, even though the character is female. An idea struck me. As the class finished, I went up to Ms. Simmons' desk.

"Ms. Simmons," I said. She looked at me over her horn-rimmed glasses.

"Damien," she said back. I smiled.

"So about the musical. I know it sounds crazy, but hear me out."

Ms. Simmons smiled and said, "Well, I do like crazy. What's your idea?"

I took a breath. "Would it be possible for me to audition for the role of Carrie? I know the character is female originally, but I think it would be really interesting if we did a gender-bent queer remake of the play."

Ms. Simmons was silent for a moment as she considered this. "It's not a bad idea, especially with how diverse it would make the story." She was silent for a moment. "Tell you what. If your audition is good enough, good enough to beat out the other girls, I'll consider it."

I almost squealed. "Thank you so much! I'll get to work on it right away."

I turned to leave the class but bumped into someone. "Oh, sorry!" I looked up and gasped. It's *him*. The hot asshole.

He raised an eyebrow. "You should watch where you're going."

I frowned. "Hmph. Don't tell me what to do." As I walked away I turned around and I thought to myself, *what a weirdo.*

Then I remembered that we'd have to perform our scene next week. And that I still haven't even picked one out. I groaned and turned back around to Ms. Simmons's classroom, hoping Alec would still be there. Just as I opened the door, it opened and there he was. Alec raised another eyebrow.

"Back for more?" he asked.

I frowned. "Listen. Meet me at Starbucks in an hour. We need to talk about our scene." Alec opened his mouth to reject me, but I cut him off. "Look. I know you don't like me and I know you don't want to do this scene. But I'm not going to get a bad grade because of a jerkwad like you!" There was silence. And then get this. For the first time, the bastard *smiled.* And oh, god. His smile was captivating. He had dimples when he smiled which made him look even more hot.

"Jerkwad?" he asked, still smiling.

I collected myself. "Yes, that's exactly what you are. I'll see you in an hour."

And then I walked away from the jerkwad.

I was sitting at a Starbucks table an hour later. Of course this guy wasn't on time. Either that, or he wasn't gonna show up at all. I wouldn't be surprised. I was sipping my pink Frappuccino and reading scenes from plays when I looked up and saw Alec.

"Wow," I said. "You actually showed up."

Alec smiled another infuriating smile. "I can leave if you prefer that."

I rolled my eyes. "Please just sit. I don't want to be here anymore than you do."

Alec sat down and looked at my pink Frappuccino. "Seriously? A Frappuccino?"

I glared at him. "What's wrong with Frappuccinos? They're delicious!" I exclaimed.

He laughed. "Yeah, I prefer just coffee."

I smiled wryly. "Lemme guess. Black with no sugar or cream?"

His eyes glimmered. "Of course." And then there was silence.

I cleared my throat. "Um, so. I was reading through scenes and I thought this might be a good one." I pushed a paper at him. He picked it up and began to read. I took a sip from my insulted Frappuccino. He put the paper down.

"It's a romance scene," he said.

I narrowed my eyes. "Yeah, those are usually good ones." There was silence.

"Unless…you're uncomfortable with that. I know we're both guys, so…" I sighed.

He tilted his head. "That's not an issue for me."

"Oh…so you're fine with this scene?" I asked, taken aback.

He looked at me with those intense blue eyes. "Yeah, it's fine," he said finally.

"I know you hate me, but just try and pretend you don't for the scene, alright?" I looked at him seriously.

"I…I don't hate you." Alec fidgeted with his sleeve. I stared at him, waiting for him to continue. "I just…I'm not that great. With people, I mean." He looked away from me. And something strange was going on in my chest. I didn't know what it was. Suddenly, I wanted to know everything about this person. And I didn't even know why. I realized he was waiting for me to respond, but I was at a loss.

"It's alright," I finally said.

"It is?" he asked, surprised.

"Yeah, it is. As long as you stop acting like a jerkwad, I think I can handle it." I smiled. Then Alec smiled genuinely and I almost melted right then and there. I blushed and quickly looked away, hoping he didn't notice. "W-we should probably just read through the scene," I said. He nodded slowly and we began the first read through. Alec was actually a better actor than I thought. I suddenly had hope that our scene would go well. After a couple more read-throughs, we decided to stop for the day. When he got up to leave, I said, "Alec, wait." He turned around, waiting for me to speak. But then I was unsure of what I wanted to say. "I…I hope you have a good day," I finished lamely. He just nodded and walked away. I just stood there, watching his figure grow smaller and smaller until he was gone completely. Maybe this Alec guy wasn't as bad as I thought he was.

It's trying to break free but it cannot.

It's struggling and trying and pleading, but it cannot see the light.

It's dark and it's cold. It's musty, and it's been this way for years and years and years.

The seal is too strong, but it can feel it growing weaker every day.

One day it will break free. It senses it.

And it will cause destruction to the one who sealed it away.

The former Prince of Krusada.

CHAPTER 3

I broke the promise I had made to myself and I went to see Prince Alec again. After my studies, I told the guards I was going for a ride on my horse and I'd be back soon. I walked outside wearing a pale lavender cloak and breathed in the fresh air. It was a clear, sunny day and there were pure white clouds in the sky. I went to the stables and I saddled up Lola, who looked delighted to see me. I swung my leg over her and then we were off.

We traveled to the castle of Dynalis and I was already excited to see him again. As we got closer to the castle, I saw guards. I made a sharp turn to prevent them from seeing me, then directed Lola to behind the castle. I hoped that Alec was in the gardens again. I tied Lola to a nearby tree and I walked onto the grounds of the garden. Disappointment settled in me when I didn't see him. I walked into the gazebo and admired the beautiful flowers and plants surrounding it. I wondered if he planted all of these himself. I picked up a lone fallen flower on the ground and I inhaled its sweet scent. I pulled my hood over my head, deciding to leave before I was seen by the guards or anyone else.

"I was hoping you'd come back." I turned around completely and there he was, smiling at me. I returned the smile, and I lowered my hood.

"I was beginning to think you wouldn't show," I said.

"Are you here for that tour I promised?" He took the flower from me and put it behind my ear. He smiled, his eyes crinkling. "Beautiful." I blushed and I looked away. He extended his hand to me. "Come. Let me show you the castle of Dynalis."

We entered the castle and I was astonished. I knew the castle was bigger than my own, but this was…something else. As we walked down an enormous hallway, I saw huge golden chandeliers and windows that let in the sun, the floor made of brown marble, and the walls covered in beautiful, ornate golden wallpaper. We entered another room and I gasped. Inside was a gorgeous ballroom. There were massive chandeliers everywhere, the floor was covered with gold in hexagonal patterns, and there were huge mirrors, also gold, lining the walls. I looked up and I saw a beautiful painting of clouds and a blue sky. It was one of the most stunning rooms I had ever seen. We walked down the grand steps and onto the floor that I assumed was for parties and dancing. Alec turned to me.

"So. What do you think?" I shook my head, unable to put into words what I was thinking. He laughed. "Speechless, I see."

"It's beautiful. Truly, I'm impressed."

He looked around the room and said, "This room is used only for the most elaborate parties and dances." He turned to me and extended his hand. "May I have this dance?"

"I'm terrible at dancing," I laughed.

He grinned. "Don't worry, I'll lead. You just follow me."

I sighed. "But there's no music."

Really, I was just trying to make excuses so I didn't have to dance. He considered this and then walked to the far side of the ballroom, where of course there was a big gramophone mounted to the wall. He picked up a dusty record lying beside it. A moment later I heard the tune of "Moonlight Sonata" by Beethoven playing. My eyes widened. I loved this song. Alec walked back toward me and extended his hand again. I swallowed and I reluctantly took it.

Suddenly we were moving, my hand in his hand and my other hand on his shoulder. We spun in circles and I felt like I was in a dream. Alec was an amazing dancer, which isn't surprising. He spun me around and I smiled like an idiot. We danced like this for a while, then he pulled me in to rest my head against his chest. I could feel his heartbeat. I never wanted this moment to end. I wished that time would stop right now, forever. After a bit, he pulled back. He smiled, his eyes glittering.

"See? You're not that bad at all."

I smiled and I said, "That's only because you were leading."

He laughed, "Maybe."

I took a breath in. "Thank you."

Alec crinkled his nose in confusion. "For what?"

I looked around and lifted my shoulders up and down. "Just...for everything. Really." He smiled and stepped in closer.

"I realize that this is only the second time we've met, but I want to know more about you. All I know is your name and that you like to trespass in other peoples' gardens."

I looked away and I felt sad because I knew I couldn't tell him the truth. How my true name is Damien, Prince Damien of Krusada. That I was supposed to be his enemy and that I shouldn't even be here. "The truth is...I'm just the son of a nobleman. I...I reside in the country of Agatonia."

Agatonia is a neighboring country to the kingdom of Dynalis. Alec nodded slowly. "I see. Well, Dimitri. I'm glad to know at least a little more about you." Guilt flooded my body.

I cleared my throat. "I'm needed back at home and I should probably return."

He nodded and led me back out to the gardens where Lola was waiting for me. Alec grinned and began to pet Lola's mane.

"What a beautiful girl you are." I smiled at this and I told him her name. Alec turned to me as I got on Lola. "There is something I want to ask you. In two days, there will be a party in the ballroom, a celebration for my twenty-first birthday. I wanted to invite you." I was stunned by this. I'd love to go, but was it even possible? I wasn't sure.

"I…I'll try and make it." He seemed satisfied by my answer, then Lola and I were off, and I already missed him.

Present Day, New York

Alec

I saw what looked like a huge castle. It's a beautiful castle made of marble and gold. I could see a silhouette on the balcony. It was hard to make out, but I saw a man—a man wearing a white hooded cloak and he was trying to tell me something, but it was so hard to hear. I strained to hear him and suddenly I could make out part of what he was saying:

"Find him or this world will be destroyed."

I woke up with a start, soaked in sweat. I breathed heavily and gasped for air. I got up and I looked out my window. All I saw was darkness and cars passing by. I kept having the same dream and visions over and over. What do they mean? I was unsure. But I did know one thing for sure:

I had found him.

CHAPTER 4

Present Day, New York

Damien

After class, I asked Ms. Simmons if Alec and I could use the space to start blocking our scene. She gave us permission, so it was just Alec and me in the room. I had most of my lines memorized and we went over how to block the scene. It wasn't a very complicated scene; most of the time we were just sitting opposite each other at a table. After we rehearsed a couple of times, I bemoaned to him how I haven't even started prepping my audition for the musical, which was next week.

"Oh, yeah. You're auditioning for the role of Carrie, right?" he asked.

"Yeah, how did you know?"

He blushed a little, which I found incredibly cute. "I overheard you ask Ms. Simmons the other day."

I nodded, "Yeah. I've always loved the original book and film. And I've always dreamed of playing Carrie. Even though the character is female, I asked Ms. Simmons if I could maybe do a gender-bent version."

"I've been thinking…" Alec said. Then he looked away and didn't finish his sentence.

"Thinking what?" I asked.

Alec shook his head. "Nothing, it's stupid."

I tilted my head. "It's probably not stupid. Tell me."

Alec sighed. "I was thinking of auditioning for the play too."

That's not what I was expecting him to say. "Oh…for what part?" I asked.

"Tommy Ross."

I was especially taken aback by this because Tommy was a pretty important character in the play. Not only that, but he's the one who takes Carrie to prom.

"Oh. Wow." I thought about this. "Well, I mean if you want to audition then I think you should just do it."

Alec shifted in his seat. "It's just, I've never actually acted in a play before."

I considered this and said, "Well, you never know until you try, right?"

Alec shrugged. "I guess so."

"So. Where did you transfer from, anyways? I've never asked you that."

Alec fidgeted and looked out the window. "I…came from a school in Pennsylvania."

I nodded slowly and then I asked, "Oh, do your parents live in Pennsylvania too?"

Then there was silence and I realized I may have overstepped. "I…you don't have to answer that. I'm being nosy, sorry," I said quickly.

Alec shook his head. "It's fine. Both of my parents aren't around anymore."

My stomach dropped and I looked at him. "I'm sorry…I-I didn't realize."

Alec shrugged like it was no big deal. "It's fine," he said.

Silence again.

Alec looked at me. "So, I've answered your questions. What about you? What's your story?"

I smiled a little and I explained how I was an only child and that my father lives in Brooklyn. I told him how I've always wanted to go to NYU and pursue acting.

"Wow," Alec said. "So your dream came true."

I shrugged sheepishly and said, "Well, sort of. I'm still not on Broadway or anything, so."

Alec laughed a little at this. I picked up our script. An idea came into my head and I looked at Alec. "So, I think we've got our scene down pretty well. I was thinking…if you want to, would you like to audition for *Carrie* together?"

Alec looked surprised. "Are you sure?"

I nodded. "Yeah, I'm sure. I think it would be fun."

Alec smiled shyly. "Alright," he said. Suddenly, I felt excited about this and I suggested that we meet at my dorm tomorrow to start preparing for our audition and he agreed. This should be interesting.

"What the fuck?" Karina was looking at me, shocked. We were sitting at our usual table at Starbucks and I was spilling all the tea. I sipped from my usual pink Frappuccino.

"What?!" I asked defensively.

Karina scoffed. "Well, it's just so *weird*. One minute you hate the guy and now you're auditioning for a musical together?"

I shrugged. "Well, he's not as bad as I thought he was. I think he's more misunderstood than anything."

Karina gave me a look. "Oh, Damien. You always want to see the best in people, don't you?"

I shrugged again. "I just don't think he's as bad as I thought."

Karina leaned back in her chair. "Well, alright, if you say so."

I shifted in my seat. "Also…I sort of invited him over to rehearse tomorrow."

Karina's eyes widened. "You did what?!"

I lifted my hands up defensively. "We need to practice for the audition! It's next week and I…I just said it without thinking."

Karina took a sip from her vanilla latte. "Clearly," she said. She thought for a moment and said, "Well, I guess it's fine. I'll go study in the courtyard or something while you two…do whatever."

I gave her a big smile and said, "Thank you! I really appreciate it."

Karina rolled her eyes. "Yeah, yeah. I'm the best, I know."

I laughed and took a sip from my drink, still thinking about Alec and his unusual personality.

Tomorrow eventually came and Karina kept her promise about leaving the dorm room so Alec and I could practice. I realized I still didn't have Alec's phone number, but I did tell him what room I live in and what time to come over, so I just hoped he remembered. Eventually, I heard a knock. I double checked my reflection in the mirror before opening it.

There Alec stood, wearing black jeans and an oversized maroon hoodie with his signature black Vans. I smiled and let him in. He looked around at the room, from the two twin beds to the white ceiling to the wooden bookshelf by my bed.

"Nice room," he said.

"Thanks," I replied.

I sat down on my bed and gestured for him to sit next to me. He seemed embarrassed but sat down. "So, I know part of the audition is to sing a clip from a song from the musical," I explained. "Obviously we'll sing our own separate songs." He nodded along as I talked about how we also need to do a read through of a brief scene from the show. I gave him the idea of doing the scene where Carrie and Tommy first arrive at prom and he asks her to dance. Alec nodded.

"Yeah, I think that's a good scene."

"Cool. I'll go print the scenes out for us then," I said.

I grabbed my laptop and printed out the scene. I handed Alec his copy and our hands brushed for a split second. My heartbeat quickened. "So, let's just read it through. Let's start at the part where Tommy asks Carrie to dance."

Alec nodded and began reading the first line. We went back and forth and it felt really natural for just the first read through. We got to the part where Carrie and Tommy finally do get up and dance after voting themselves prom king and queen.

I looked at Alec. "So…how did that feel?"

Alec nodded. "Yeah, that felt good. I think you chose a good scene."

I blushed and looked away. "Thank you. Yeah, it felt like it flowed really well for just the first time. And the blocking is super simple since we're just sitting the whole time. I guess we just need to work on memorizing the lines."

We read through a couple more times before we decided to stop for the day.

"Oh! What was your number? I realize I never got it," I said.

Alec gave me his number and I gave him mine. Alec got up to leave and I followed him to the door. Before he left, he stopped to look at my overflowing bookcase.

"Wow…that's a lot of books."

I laughed. "Yeah, I like to read a lot." Alec picked up a used copy of *The Song of Achilles*.

"Oh, yeah…I loved that one. It's a tragedy about these lovers who couldn't be together on Earth, but they find each other again in death." I smiled faintly. "Romantic, huh?"

Alec nodded. "Yeah, it is." He looked as though we wanted to say something else but then gingerly set the book down and headed for the door.

"Thanks again for coming over," I said. Alec just nodded and said goodbye. I closed the door and felt lightheaded. I went to lie down and I thought to myself that our audition would be good. I really hoped I got the part. Now it was time to practice my song, but maybe I should take a quick nap first…

A long time ago
The night of the party

Tonight was Prince Alec's birthday celebration, and I was pacing the floors of my chamber wondering if I should make an appearance. I wanted to, of course I wanted to. But since it was late in the night, I would have to sneak out of the castle. I was still pacing when I ultimately decided to go. I so desperately want to see him again. I thought he would be disappointed if I was not there, at least briefly. I opened my wooden closet and picked out my finest silk robes, the color of the night sky. I chose a dark blue cloak with little stars embroidered on it and I looked at my reflection. Tan skin, brown wavy hair, and brown eyes looked back at me. I decided I looked decent and I slowly opened the door and entered the hallway. I had to make sure my father didn't catch me; typically he was away in his room and I didn't see much of him, especially after my mother passed years prior. I quietly creeped down the stairs and then I successfully entered the outside world.

Lola and I rode to the kingdom of Dynalis. As we neared the castle, I saw a huge crowd. I had forgotten this was the prince's celebration. Of course there would be a huge number of guests attending, probably other royalty and upper class citizens. I was unsure how I

children, as would I. I was lost in thought for a while when I heard footsteps behind me. I turned around and it was Alec. I turned back around and I didn't say anything. He stood next to me.

"Beautiful view, isn't it?" he asked. I nodded because it was a beautiful view. I saw tall mountains in the distance and sparkling stars in the sky, just like the ones on my cloak. Alec turned to me. "Are you…upset with me?"

"Why would you think that?" I asked.

Alec looked down. "You left before the dinner was even served."

"I wasn't hungry," I shrugged.

Alec nudged me. "Come on now. I know it is more than that."

I sighed and I looked him in the eye. "Is there a beautiful lady in your life?"

Alec looked completely taken aback at this. "What are you talking about?" he asked.

I looked away. "I heard rumors that there is a lady you want to marry."

Alec was silent for a moment, then he began to laugh.

I narrowed my eyes at him. "What's so funny?"

He stopped laughing and said, "Sorry. It's just…it's adorable when you're jealous."

I gaped and I exclaimed to him, "I-I'm not jealous! I just…I don't even know what this is. What we are."

Alec nodded and he leaned in close to me and I could feel his warm breath. "This is what we are."

And then he kissed me under the moonlight.

We kissed and I closed my eyes. His lips gently brushed against mine and it tasted so sweet. He pulled away slowly and looked at me.

"Does that answer your question?" he asked. I looked away and smiled.

"Maybe a little," I said.

CHAPTER 5

Present Day, New York

Damien

Next week arrived before I knew it, and it was the day of the auditions. I was nervous, but I thought Alec and I were ready. We had been practicing our scene a lot and I'd been practicing my song as well. I entered the auditorium and saw Alec sitting there already, along with a lot of other people. My stomach flipped. I didn't realize this many people would be auditioning. *It's ok,* I told myself. *It'll be fine.* I sat down next to Alec.

"Are you ready?" I asked.

He nodded reluctantly. "I think so. But I'm nervous."

I smiled. "Me too. But I think we're gonna do great."

He nodded again and then Ms. Simmons entered the auditorium. She was wearing a brown sweater dress with a gray cap on her red hair. She smiled and thanked everybody for coming to audition, then explained that we would go in order of the sign-up sheet. At this, my heartbeat quickened. I knew I'd be one of the first to go. When my turn came to perform my song, I took a deep breath and I walked up the stage. Although I was nervous, I also felt liberated being on stage. Something about it made me feel at home.

"Hello! My name is Damien and I'll be performing the song 'Why Not Me?'"

I looked at the pianist sitting at the corner of the stage and nodded that I was ready. She began to play and I began singing. As I sang, I couldn't help but focus on Alec. I was unsure why, but I felt less nervous when I looked at him. He smiled and nodded along, like he was encouraging me to keep going. The song was almost done, and I sang the finishing lyrics.

Everyone clapped and I smiled and left the stage. I thought my song went well, but I still needed to perform the scene with Alec. When it was Alec's turn to sing, he walked onto the stage and smiled shyly. His shy smile was so freaking cute I could have melted right then and there.

"Hi. My name is Alec and I'll be singing 'Dreamer in Disguise.'"

And then he started singing. I was floored. His voice was beautiful. It was deep and alluring and masculine in a sexy way. Eventually, he finished and I clapped loudly because he did a great job and I couldn't help but feel proud of him. Alec sat back down next to me and I whispered, "You never told me you could sing like that!" and he shrugged modestly and smiled. A couple of other people went up to sing but they were nowhere near as good as Alec was.

Eventually it was time for Alec and me to perform our scene. We recited our lines just like we did in rehearsal, and I thought it went well. Ms. Simmons seemed pleased with our read through and thanked us. We sat back down and I told Alec he did a great job.

"Thanks. You too," he said.

I sat back down and watched the rest of the auditions. Maybe I'm biased, but none of them were as good as Alec and me were.

At the end of the week, the audition results were finally posted. I almost sprinted to the auditorium to see the paper posted on the door. I took a breath and read. Then I almost died right then and there because:

CARRIE WHITE..................Damien Jones

TOMMY ROSS.................Alec Caldwell

And that is all I read before I sprinted away, almost screaming. I must have looked like a madman because I almost knocked right into a freshman girl. I whipped my cell phone out of my pocket and I quickly texted Alec.

OMG! You'll never believe this! We got cast in the musical!!

Alec replied a minute later.

Woah, no way! I'm in shock right now. That's awesome! ☺

And it was so cute because he sent a little smiley emoji. I smiled dumbly at my phone. I was so excited and happy that it didn't hit me until I get back to my dorm and then I remembered:

Oh shit. We're gonna have to kiss.

A long time ago
The first time

After the party, I snuck out of the castle various times to see Alec. We did different things together. Sometimes we just sat in the garden and talked. I told him about my love for reading and he showed me the library which had hundreds, if not thousands, of books in it. Other times, we wandered the castle and Alec would show me different rooms. Today was different though; we were in a boat, rowing together on a lake nearby Dynalis. It was nighttime and I could hear crickets chirping. Alec smiled at me.

"What do you think of the lake?"

"It's beautiful." I looked up and saw a full moon shining above.

"You're beautiful," Alec said. My heart felt like it was going to burst out of my chest.

I looked at Alec. "You said you wanted to know more about me. I want to know more about you."

"Ask away."

I thought for a moment. "What's your family like?"

Silence. I realized I might have asked the wrong question.

Alec sighed. "I've never exactly had a big family. My parents both died when I was a boy. So, I live with my uncle who is the current king of Dynalis."

I looked down and said, "I'm so sorry."

Alec shrugged like it was no big deal.

I told him about how my mother passed when I was a child. I told him how I was very close to her and that she was very warm and kind. I even showed him my necklace. It's a heart shaped locket that belonged to my mother. "It's the only thing I have left of her," I said. He nodded and took my hands in his. His hands were bigger than mine but they felt so warm.

"Thank you for trusting me and for telling me that." I smiled and nodded.

Alec looked around and asked if we should head back to the castle. I nodded and said that was a good idea, even though I didn't want our date to end.

We headed back to the castle and Alec asked if he could show me something. I nodded and he led me upstairs to a room on the far end of the hallway. He opened the door to a room I'd never been in before. It was a beautiful room with purple silk draping the walls. There was a bed and a tall wooden bookcase with many books on it. I realized that this must be his private chambers. I blushed at this and he led me in.

"Are you sure it's alright for me to be here?" I asked tentatively.

Alec smiled. "Of course. It's my room after all."

I looked around the room and stood there dumbly. Alec turned to me and had a serious expression on his face. "Listen. I know we haven't known each other for very long. And the truth is, I don't let in people that easily." He looked away. "I haven't felt like this about anyone before. That day I saw you in my garden, I felt like the world was bestowing me a gift."

I blushed again and looked away. And I felt a tremendous amount of guilt because I still hadn't told him the truth about myself. "I… feel the same way," I said.

Alec stepped in close and lightly lifted up my chin. I looked up at his crystal clear blue eyes as he leaned in and our lips touched. But this kiss felt different than our first kiss, which was so gentle and light. This kiss is deeper and more demanding. I could feel his tongue enter my mouth and our tongues connect with each other. Alec put his hand on my hips and I put my arms around his broad shoulders. We kissed for a bit longer, our tongues exploring each other's mouths and then Alec finally pulled back, a string of saliva connecting our mouths before it broke apart.

Alec looked at me and I realized there must be a strange expression on my face because he asked me what was wrong. I looked away and stayed silent.

"Do you…did you not like it?" he asked quietly.

I quickly looked at him and said, "No! I…I really liked it! It's just…I have something to tell you. And I fear you might never want to see me again when I tell you."

Alec looked at me seriously and reassured me that would never happen, regardless of what I told him. I sighed and sat down on the edge of his bed.

"I…the truth is, my name isn't Dimitri." Alec stayed silent and nodded and waited for me to continue. "My real name is… Damien. And I'm…the prince of Krusada."

Silence. I looked at Alec, my heart racing and he was looking at the wall, his expression unreadable. Alec finally turned and looked at me.

"I had a feeling you weren't telling me the complete truth. And if I'm being completely honest…I had a sneaking suspicion that you were the prince of Krusada."

I looked at him, shocked. "How did you know?" I asked.

Alec looked at me and said, "Your accent tipped me off a little. And…I had heard rumors of the prince's beauty. I smiled at this comment. I then sighed and looked down.

"So…you aren't mad?" I asked.

Alec shook his head and sat next to me. "No, I'm not mad. I understand why you had to lie. I'm just glad you told me."

I looked at him and said, "You really are the best. Thank you for understanding."

Alec leaned in and kissed my cheek. "There's nothing you can say that would ever make me hate or dislike you," he whispered.

I wanted to cry because I was so touched to hear this. I looked up at him and kissed him. We kissed violently and soon our tongues were exploring again. After a moment, he pulled us apart and rested his forehead against mine.

"Do you…want to?" he whispered.

I nodded. I had never been more sure of anything in my life. He began to kiss my neck and I let out a soft moan. He began untying my robes and I shrugged them off, now only in my undergarments and undershirt. I laid down on the bed and he climbed on top of me, still fully clothed. He resumed kissing my neck and I sighed. He then trailed a hand down my torso and caressed my thigh. Alec took my undershirt off and I suddenly felt self-conscious. Alec seemed to recognize this because he looked at me and said, "Don't worry. You're beautiful."

I almost cried at this statement. Alec began to tease and lick my pink nipple and I groaned. My nipples were very sensitive and he seemed to pick up on this quickly. He softly bit them and continued to lick and explore them with his tongue. He was still caressing my thighs and then suddenly I felt his large hand on my hardening bulge. My hips almost involuntarily jumped up and he began feeling and stroking my penis over my undergarments. It felt amazing and my cock was already fully hard. I could see that there is also a spot of liquid forming on my undergarments as well.

"This feel good?" Alec asked. I just nodded, still breathing heavily. Then he finally slipped my undergarments off and my hard cock sprung out like it was waiting for this. Alec took me in his hand and began softly stroking me. I moaned because it felt so good, unlike anything I've ever felt before. Pleasuring myself felt nothing like this. And then I suddenly gasped because Alec had taken me in his mouth. I could feel his hot mouth on my cock and he was licking and teasing the head with his warm tongue. Then he went deeper and bobbed his head up and down, taking the full length like an expert. I was breathing heavily and I didn't know how much more I could take. He caressed my balls with one hand with my cock still in his mouth. Then Alec focused on the head again, his tongue teasing the slit of my cock.

I could feel something hot spreading through me and I tried to warn him, tried to tell him that I could feel my climax approaching. He seemed to pick up on this because he bobbed his head faster, taking my full length again and suddenly I was crying out and I felt myself emptying into him. Alec swallowed professionally and lifted up, looking at me. There was a bit of silence as I recovered.

Then Alec laid next to me. "How was it?"

Still breathing heavily, I looked at him and I said, "That was…amazing. Much better than stroking myself at home." Alec laughed at this. Then I realized he was still clothed.

"I want to make you feel good too," I said.

He grinned and said, "Oh, really?" I nodded and I kissed him, and I began to disrobe him. I untied his robes and vest, and then he was shirtless and I was shocked. I knew Alec was strong, but he had such a chiseled body I was amazed. I ran a hand up his hard hairy chest and down his abdominal muscles, feeling the dark hair scattered across his body. I ran a thumb over his hard nipples, taking it all in. I lowered my hands slowly and unzipped his pants and took off his under-garments. His cock sprung out and I loved that he was already hard as a rock.

I was again shocked because his cock was huge. It was pale, just like the color of Alec's skin with a large mushroom shaped head that was darker in color. Definitely a cock fitting of a future king. I took him in my hand and stroked him a little, experimenting to see what he liked. I could see him close his eyes and moan softly. After stroking him for a bit I decided to just go for it and I took him in my mouth.

Alec cried out and I caressed his large balls in my hand. I licked and teased his head and dug my tongue into his slit. I tried to take his length but he was a bit big for me. I tried my best anyway because I wanted to make him feel good. I bobbed my head up and down on his manhood and I licked his shaft with my tongue at the same time. Alec was making unintelligible noises, so I thought I must be doing something right. And then suddenly I felt his hand on the back of my head and he began to face-fuck me. He thrusted in and out of my mouth and I had my hands around his ass.

"So fucking good," he moaned. And then he gently stopped and pulled his cock from my mouth, a string of saliva connecting us. Alec was breathing heavily and in between breaths he said, "Need to be inside you."

I nodded eagerly because I wanted this as well. He grabbed a bottle of oil from the dresser and began to lube up his hard giant cock. He told me to lay on my back and I did. He towered above me and looked me in the eyes.

"This…may hurt a bit. I'll be as gentle as I can."

I nodded and closed my eyes. I then felt his head press against my entrance, the oil dripping down my ass. Then, all of a sudden, I felt his large head pop in and I gasped. Alec asked if I was alright and I nodded. Alec pushed in more until his full length was inside me. It burned and I felt like I was being split open. The pain also felt good and I was so happy we were finally connected, our bodies as one.

Alec smiled and asked, "Is it alright if I move?"

I nodded. Alec softly began to pull out and then thrust back in and I moaned loudly. Alec grinned at this and began to thrust into me, and we fell into a good rhythm. My legs were spread open, and my feet were on his broad shoulders. He kissed me deeply as he thrusted into me and I could feel his cock hitting my prostate with every thrust.

"You're fucking beautiful," Alec growled and I felt like I was in heaven. After a while of more thrusting and kissing, Alec pulled slowly out and ordered me to get on my hands and knees which I quickly did. Alec pushed his fat cock in again and started fucking me like this. He put his hands on my shoulders and moved his hips in and out, going at a faster pace with each thrust.

Eventually Alec grunted, "Gonna come, gonna come deep inside you."

Then a couple moments later, I could feel him spill his seed inside me, it gushing out of my ass. Alec breathed heavily and rested his head against my back, recovering from his climax. Alec slowly pulled out and I lay down on my back, ass throbbing. Alec laid next to me and asked if that was okay, and if I was feeling alright.

I nodded, catching my breath. "That was incredible. You were amazing. It was like…seeing a different side of you."

Alec grinned and asked if he was too rough or harsh and I quickly said no. "I like it when you take control," I said shyly.

Alec laughed and kissed me.

I love this man, I thought to myself.

It can finally sense the light.

The time is drawing near for its escape.

It can feel the seal begin to crack and deteriorate.

It just needs to find its former host.

The former King of Krusada.

CHAPTER 6

Present Day, New York

Damien

Ms. Simmons let us know rehearsals for *Carrie* would begin after winter break. I couldn't believe fall had already passed and winter break was approaching. At the same time, I was excited to see my father again. After class, I saw Alec start to leave the room. I took a deep breath and walked up to him and called his name.

Alec turned around. "Oh, hey. What's up?"

I fidgeted with my sweater sleeve and I decided it's now or never. "So…I realize that the only times we've hung out are, like, to work on acting projects."

Alec nodded and waited for me to continue. I cleared my throat and said, "Well…I-I was wondering if you, like, maybe wanted to…hang out…just for fun?"

There was a beat of silence and then Alec grinned. "Are you…asking me out on a date?"

My eyes widened because…*am I?* "No! I mean…maybe?" I said hesitantly.

Alec considered this for a moment and then said, "Okay, yeah. I'm down."

I was stunned. I didn't think he would really say yes. "Oh, cool! Um…I was thinking maybe we could walk around Central Park and maybe grab some coffee or something?"

Alec gave me another beautiful smile. "Yeah, that sounds cool."

I nodded. "Does tomorrow sound good?"

He agreed. I was stunned at myself. I never thought I'd have the balls to ask out a guy before—let alone the guy actually say yes. When we went our separate ways, I texted Karina to meet me at Starbucks.

"Soo…I have some major news," I started off.

Karina was wearing a navy blue sweater and dark jeans with her blond hair in a messy bun. She grinned and said, "I heard! Congratulations on the musical!" I was actually referring to Alec and I going on a date, but I nodded anyway.

"Thank you! I'm super excited for it! But, that's actually not what I was gonna tell you."

Karina tilted her head. "No?" she asked.

I shook my head. "I sort of have, might have asked Alec on a date."

Now Karina's jaw dropped. "You're kidding. *Asshole Alec?*"

I gave her a look. "He's not an asshole, he's just a little shy. But yeah, and he said yes!"

Karina shook her head. "Wow…that's really exciting. I'm happy for you," she said.

"It's really the first date I've ever had so I'm kind of nervous," I confessed.

Karina smiled reassuringly. "Damien. You're super-hot and one of the friendliest people I know. *Alec* should be the one who is nervous."

And this is why I loved Karina. I honestly don't know what I'd do without her.

"So," she said, setting down her latte. "What are your plans for winter break?"

I told Karina how I was going to Brooklyn to stay with my dad. Karina told me how she was going back home to San Diego to visit family. We talked for a bit more before we went our separate ways.

Tomorrow rolled around and I was supposed to meet Alec at Central Park. It was chilly out, so I wore my favorite red peacoat with dark jeans and Doc Marten boots. I put on my seahorse necklace and I headed out. The walk to Central Park wasn't too far, and by the time I got there, I saw Alec waiting for me.

"Alec!" I called out. He turned around and smiled. He looked adorable in his black hoodie and had rosy cheeks from the cold. I could've kissed him right then and there.

"Shall we?" I said and he nodded. We walked toward the coffee shop nearby and I asked him how his day was so far.

"It's been alright," he said. I told him the same and we eventually made it to the coffee shop. We ordered and then sat down. We were at a cafe called Bluestone Lane, a pretty modern looking place with fluorescent lights, wooden chairs, and cushioned booths. We sat at a booth and there was silence—but it wasn't awkward silence. I felt at ease just being with Alec even if we're not talking.

Alec pointed to my necklace. "You always wear that. Does it mean anything?" he asked.

I touched my pendant and was quiet for a moment. "It was a gift. From my mother, before she passed," I explained.

Alec nodded. "Oh. It's really pretty."

I smiled and said, "Thank you."

Just then, our order arrived. Alec just got black coffee and I got something sugary and sweet with whipped cream. Alec stirred his coffee and I could feel like he wanted to ask me something but was afraid to.

"What is it?" I asked.

Alec looked out one of the windows and he paused. "Have you…do you ever have any odd dreams?"

I was taken aback because this was the last thing I expected him to say. I tilted my head. "What do you mean?"

Alec shook his head and said, "Nevermind. That was a weird question, I'm sorry."

I thought for a moment and said, "Well, I've never really had any weird dreams…usually I forget them by the time I wake up."

Alec nodded. Then, I felt a strong wave of familiarity, like I'd been in this situation before. But I couldn't place when or why. I decided to steer the conversation in a different direction and I asked Alec what his plans are for break. Alec just shrugged and said he didn't really have any plans. I considered this when a crazy idea popped into my brain.

"Hey…If you don't have any plans, would you want to visit my dad with me?"

Alec looked up, surprised by this invitation. "Oh, no. I couldn't impose like that."

I shook my head. "You wouldn't be imposing. Seriously, it would be fun! And we have a guest room you can stay in and I know my dad would be cool with it."

Alec was silent. "Are you sure?" he asked.

I nodded. "I'm sure."

Alec looked at me. "Okay" he said.

I smiled. "Awesome."

Winter break came faster than I expected. I texted Alec to meet me at my dorm at 8:00 a.m. and that we'd take a taxi to get to my house. I was nervous but excited. I thought my dad would really like Alec. And it would be great seeing my dad again. Morning arrived, and I brushed my teeth and took a warm shower. Afterwards, I put on a navy blue cardigan with star shaped buttons and a pair of light blue jeans. I made sure I had everything packed away and I put my bag of luggage and backpack to the side. Karina had already left for San Diego and texted me saying she got there safely.

A moment later, I heard a knock at the door and I opened it. There he was, wearing black fitted jeans and a red and black striped sweater. He looked adorable in it. He had a backpack and one duffel bag.

I smiled. "Are you ready?" He nodded yes and we walked out to the front doors together. We waved for a taxi and we were able to flag one down. I told the driver the address and we were off. In the taxi, Alec looked out the window at the passing cars and trees.

"Have you lived in New York your whole life?" Alec asked and I shook my head.

"We moved here after my mother passed. Wanted a fresh start, I guess. So I think I've lived here since I was, like, twelve?" Alec just nodded and kept looking out the window. It took us about forty minutes to get there and most of the time Alec and I sat in silence, aside from the music playing on the radio. Eventually, I saw the familiar shape of the apartment complex. The taxi came to a stop and I passed the driver some money. We walked up the stairs to the upper level and I pressed the buzzer for the fourth door down the hallway. A couple moments went by before my dad opened the door. He smiled when he saw me and gave me a big hug. It felt good and I was happy to be home. I loved school, but I had to admit that I'd been feeling a bit homesick recently. We pulled apart and that's when I got a better look at my dad. He was wearing cargo pants and a burgundy long sleeve. But then I noticed that his tan skin looked a bit pale, and I could see some faint bags under his green eyes.

I frowned. "Dad, you look like you haven't got any sleep in days. Are you alright?"

My dad laughed at this and said he's fine. "I just haven't had the best sleep lately," he explained.

I nodded slowly and then remembered Alec was behind me. "Oh! Dad, I told you that I was bringing a guest. This is Alec."

Alec stepped forward and held out his hand. "Hi. It's nice to meet you, Mr. Jones."

My dad laughed again and shook his hand and said, "Please, just call me Samuel."

Alec nodded shyly and we entered the apartment. It was the same as I remembered it, with brown carpet and beige walls. There were pictures on the wall of my dad and me, as well as a painting of my mother. I gave this to my father as a present one year; I didn't actually paint it, I'm not talented enough for that. Instead, I commissioned it and it came out beautifully. I felt a sense of nostalgia and a wave of melancholy every time I looked at it. Suddenly, a black shape leapt onto me and I laughed; It's our cat Luna. She is a black kitty and we'd had her for a couple of years now.

"Hi girl," I cooed and petted her black fur. It seemed like she missed me and she purred. I smiled at Alec and introduced Luna to him. He grinned and cautiously pet Luna who seemed to enjoy it.

"Alec, let me show you the guest room so you can put your stuff away," my father said and Alec nodded and followed him. I lingered in the living room for a moment with Luna and I stared up again at the painting of my mother. Her brown hair was in a side braid and her light brown eyes stared at me and she had a warm smile on her face.

"Hi, mom," I whispered. I was home.

Alec was washing up for dinner and putting his stuff away, so it was just my father and me in the kitchen for a moment. He was making my favorite: spaghetti and meatballs. It smelled delicious.

"So, how've you been kiddo?" my dad asked.

I sighed and didn't even know where to begin. "Oh, I meant to text you! I got the lead in the college musical!"

My dad grinned and clapped me on the shoulder. "Nice job! It seems like NYU recognizes talent when they see it."

I smiled and said, "Daaad."

He laughed and then switched the topic. "So, this Alec. Is this a friend, or…?" He raised his eyebrows.

I gaped and turned red. "Daaad!" I exclaimed.

My dad put his hands up defensively. "What?! I'm curious!"

I sighed and looked away. "I…I'm not sure exactly what we are yet."

My dad nodded slowly while he poured the marinara sauce into the pan. I was about to say something else when my dad dropped the spatula and clutched his head. I ran over to him and I quickly asked if he's alright.

He nodded. "It's just a migraine."

I picked up the spatula. "I'll finish dinner. You go and take some medicine and lie down."

My dad was still rubbing his head and nodded in agreement. "Yeah, yeah ok. Thank you kiddo."

Then he went to sit down on the couch where Luna curled in his lap. I finished making the spaghetti and sat the plates down. I grabbed some drinks and glasses and set them on the table. Alec entered the kitchen and I smiled.

"Dinner's ready," I said. I felt like I was a housewife for a moment, welcoming Alec home from work.

"It smells great," Alec said.

He sat down and I gave him his plate. My dad came over and I asked him if he was feeling better and he nodded.

"I think it's passed," he said.

"Have you been getting migraines a lot recently?" I asked, concerned for my dad.

He shook his head slowly and said, "Just here and there. It must be from overworking I think."

I nodded. "As long as you're sure."

We began to eat and Alec said, "This is delicious. Thank you for dinner, Mr. Jo-I mean, Sam." Alec looked a bit embarrassed.

"It's no trouble." My dad smiled.

We ate and chatted and it felt nice. I felt happy and content with this company. When we finished eating, Alec helped me put our dishes in the sink.

"I feel a bit tired so I think I'm gonna go to bed early," my dad said.

I nodded and I told dad not to overwork anymore. He smiled and said goodnight to Alec.

"Is your dad alright?" Alec asked.

I looked at the dishes. "I think so. He just seemed to have a bad migraine, although I can't remember him having those before."

Alec was quiet for a moment and we finished the dishes. "I think I'm gonna go to bed too," I said.

"I'll probably do the same," he said.

"Goodnight, Alec. I'll see you in the morning."

He smiled at me and nodded. "Goodnight, Damien."

Thump. Thump. Thump.

I woke up with a start. I heard something. A noise, like someone was banging on something. My heart quickened and I wondered if someone had broken in. I quietly got up and entered the hallway. I almost screamed when I saw another person, but it was just Alec.

"What is that?" he whispered.

I looked around. "I don't know. It sounds like it's coming from my dad's room," I whispered back.

We crept toward my dad's door and the sound got louder. I slowly opened the door and I saw…my dad. He was standing in front of the wooden cabinet in his room, rocking back and forth, letting his forehead bump against the cabinet. *Thump thump thump.* Alec looked at me.

"Is this normal?" he asked.

"Absolutely not," I said. "Dad?" I called out and he continued rocking back and forth, as if he didn't hear me. I slowly walked to my dad and could see he had his eyes closed. "Dad?" I said a bit quieter. Nothing. I breathed in, and I looked at Alec. He stared back at me, obviously spooked like I was. I gently took a hold of my father and I guided him back to bed. I laid him back down on the bed and then I pulled the covers over him. He seemed to be still sleeping, and I quietly left the room with Alec.

"Does your dad usually sleepwalk?" Alec asked. I shook my head, frightened by this encounter. Alec was quiet and we both decided to go back to bed, but I couldn't sleep for the rest of the night.

Ah yes. It can see the light and it is warm.
It has found its former host.
The man they call "Samuel."
It's waited so long
for this.

CHAPTER 7

A long time ago

The kingdom of Krusada

I quietly opened the front doors to my castle and I closed them behind me. I had come from another expedition with Prince Alec and I crept up the grand spiral staircase. I was about to enter my chambers when I heard a deep voice.

"Where were you?" I froze and my heart was in my throat. It was my father. I turned and there he was, a tall man with green eyes and wearing a black robe.

"I…" I started but didn't know what to say.

My father narrowed his eyes and said, "Don't lie to me. I'm aware you've been sneaking out of the castle for the past month."

I took a breath and I realized I was a fool to think I could've gotten away with this. He stepped in closer and I flinched. "Where. Were. You." He wasn't asking this time. I looked up and I felt the fear being replaced by anger.

"Since when do you care where I go? I never see you at all! You're always locked away in your chambers doing

God knows what! You act like I don't exist ever since mom died!" I realized I've gone a step too far. My father raised his hand and slapped me hard across the face. I was stunned, both physically and emotionally. I could feel a bit of blood trickle down my cheek.

"Remember who you're talking to," my father said before retreating to his chambers.

I stood there as he left, still in shock. After I recovered, I went into my room and I began to sob. Not just my father, but everything came crashing down on me at once. I missed my mother and her warm smile. I missed when my father actually used to talk to me and treat me like his son. I always felt so lonely...until I met him. I stopped crying for a moment and I thought about Alec. Alec, the only one who saw me for who I was. And who still loved me anyway. I thought about how it was a love that could never be and I began crying softly again. We could never wed and we could never truly be together.

And there was nothing I could do about it.

Present Day, New York

Damien

"You don't remember?" I asked, shocked.

It was the next morning and we were sitting at the kitchen table eating pancakes. My dad shook his head and asked if I was making up stuff.

I gaped and said, "Why would I lie about this? You really were sleepwalking! Alec saw it too!"

Alec nodded but didn't say anything. My dad looked down at his food, quiet for a moment.

"What is it?" I asked. I knew my dad wasn't telling me something.

"Sometimes…I do wake up in different rooms. And I can't remember anything." Silence.

I shook my head in disbelief. "So, you *have* been sleepwalking lately?" I asked.

My dad shrugged and nodded. Then he held out his arm and I gasped. There was a dark bruise on his forearm.

"Where did you get that?" I asked.

My dad shook his head and said, "It's one of those bruises you can't remember. I'm sure it's nothing."

But I wasn't so sure. We finished breakfast and Alec excused himself to the restroom. Once he was gone I asked my dad if he was sure he was alright. My dad reassured me that everything was fine and to not worry. I sighed reluctantly and nodded. I went into the living room and sat down and pet Luna, who meowed at me. After a moment, I realized that Alec hadn't returned yet. I went to see if he was in his room, but it was empty. I was about to leave when I noticed his backpack was slumped over, and stuff was spilling out of it onto the floor. I went to pick his stuff up when I noticed something strange. I knew it wasn't right of me to look in his belongings but I pulled out a photograph. It was a photograph of...*me.* It was of me walking down a corridor to class. I looked inside the backpack and I saw other photos of...me. Me having lunch in the cafeteria. Me sitting at Starbucks. The last photo scared me the most; it was an outdoor window shot of me *in my dorm.*

"What the hell are you doing!?" Alec exclaimed. I jumped and turned around. I was furious and I waved the photos.

"What the hell are *you* doing?!" I screamed back.

Alec looked at the photo and swallowed, and he stayed silent. I was so confused and flustered I could barely get the words out.

"Have you been...*stalking* me?" I asked in disbelief. More silence. I pointed to the door. "Get out. Now." Alec finally broke and he said, "Wait, Damien, please. Let me explain."

My eyes widened. "How can there be any reasonable explanation for this?!" I waved the photographs again wildly.

Alec closed his eyes and looked like he was about to cry. "Please. Just sit and I'll explain. I promise."

I stared at him and I wanted to believe him. I wanted to believe that there was a reasonable explanation for this. But how could there be? I sighed and sat down and I waited for him to speak. Alec closed the door and leaned against it.

He looked at me and asked, "Do you remember when I asked you if you had any strange dreams?"

I frowned because I wondered what this had to do with anything. Alec continued, "Well, I've been having strange dreams. And visions. Of…you."

I shook my head and I wondered if Alec had a mental disorder. "What kind of dreams?" I asked.

Alec began to pace and explained how he's been having visions and dreams of someone who looks like me issuing some sort of warning about the world being destroyed. I laughed and now I knew for sure that Alec had a mental disorder.

"Seriously? *That's* the best explanation you can come up with?"

Alec looked at me and said, "Think about it. Haven't things felt odd to you lately? I mean…even with your dad."

I narrowed my eyes and said, "What about my dad?" Alec was silent for a moment and fidgeted with his shirt.

"I just mean…I don't think any of these things are a coincidence. I think something is wrong here."

I nodded in agreement. "Yeah, there is something wrong here. *You.*"

Alec looked stunned at this and said, "You really don't believe me?"

I barked out a laugh. "Who in their right mind would believe you?!"

"You obviously are sick and need serious help."

Alec shook his head and was silent.

"Listen," I began. "You can stay here, but I'm only letting you because I'm a nice person. But once break is over and we go back I want *nothing* to do with you. And if I ever catch you stalking me again I'm going to the police."

Alec nodded. I left his room and threw the photographs on the floor.

"Keep them as a memento," I said, my voice cracking.

And then I went to my room and began to cry.

The next morning, I was sitting on the balcony by myself with a cup of hot tea. I had cried myself to sleep last night and barely slept after that fiasco. It's funny how just a couple of days ago, I was so happy eating spaghetti with my dad and Alec. Now it's all gone to shit. I took a sip of my tea when the sliding door opened. I turned to see my father.

"Mind if I join you?" he asked and I shrugged. He sat down on the chair next to me and we were both silent for a moment.

"So," my dad finally said, "Things didn't work out, huh?"

I shook my head.

My dad looked out to the view of the parking lot. "I'm sorry," he said.

I just shrugged and said, "It's fine," even though it obviously wasn't.

There was some more silence before my dad said, "But you know…just because things don't work out doesn't mean they won't get better," he said.

I looked him in the eye and said, "Trust me. It's over."

My dad sighed and said, "That bad, huh?"

I nodded and embarrassingly started to cry. My dad hugged me and suddenly I was sobbing. He hugged me and rubbed my back. After a moment I pulled back.

"Thank you," I said.

"For what?"

I shrugged. "Just for…always being there for me. Even after mom died you never neglected me and always made sure I was doing alright. I really appreciate that. You really are the best dad I could've asked for."

My dad smiled and said, "When your mother was in the hospital, she made me promise that I would always look after you. And I want you to know that no matter what happens, you can always come back to me and this apartment."

I nodded and tears trickled down my face. "I love you, Dad."

"I love you too, kiddo."

I wiped my face with my sleeve and took a deep breath. Everything would be alright. At least, that's what I told myself.

It has broken.

It enters the light.

It is free.

Destruction is coming.

CHAPTER 8

Present Day, New York

Damien

Eventually winter break came to an end and I was fucking grateful. Not that I didn't want to see my dad; it's not that. It was just so awkward since Alec and I weren't on speaking terms and we were staying in that same, small apartment. I tried to avoid him as best as I could, but of course we would run into each other. Not only that, but there were more nights of my dad sleepwalking, which woke me up and worried me. So, I haven't been getting any sleep lately. Honestly, I was ready to go back to my dorm and just resume school.

Rehearsals for *Carrie* would begin soon and I was dreading it. I would try to be as professional as I could for the sake of the project, but I was not going to talk to Alec outside of the musical. I still couldn't believe that guy was stalking me. And he wouldn't even tell me the real reason why. Instead he makes up some crazy story about the world ending. I sighed and I made sure I had everything packed away in my luggage. I put on my favorite red coat and my seahorse necklace, then entered the living room where my dad was eating toast.

"Is it that time already?" he asked.

I nodded solemnly. My dad sighed and rose from the table. He walked over and gave me a big hug.

"I'm really gonna miss you, kiddo."

I closed my eyes. "I'm really gonna miss you too, Dad."

We broke apart and he looked at me. "Make sure to take care of yourself, alright?"

"I should be saying that to you. Please. Go to a doctor and ask about the sleepwalking and bruises. I think it's important for you to get it checked out."

My dad nodded and promised he would go. I went to Luna who was sitting on the couch, curled up into a little black ball. I kissed her on the head.

"Goodbye, my sweet Luna. Please watch over Dad for me, okay?"

Luna meowed back and I was pretty sure she understood. Alec entered the room with his backpack and luggage. I swallowed and looked only at Luna. He thanked my dad for everything and they shook hands.

"I called a taxi for you guys," my dad said. "Should be here any minute."

I thanked my him and gave him one last hug. The ride back was painfully silent. I wished the Earth would just swallow me whole. After what seemed like forever, we eventually arrived back on campus. I got out and ignored Alec and I got my shit out of the trunk. I didn't even bother saying goodbye as I headed toward my dorm.

Then I heard, "Damien, wait!"

I told myself to just keep walking but something made me stop. I didn't turn around though.

"Look…I really am sorry about everything. But I just want you to know that I really am telling the truth."

Silence. I couldn't believe this guy. I shook my head in disbelief and I continued walking.

I really didn't know him at all.

I put the key into my room and entered. It was empty. I guessed Karina hadn't returned from San Diego yet, which was fine. I wanted to be alone anyways. I laid down on my bed without bothering to unpack. I thought about Alec and his blue eyes and freckles. I really was blinded by his hotness. He turned out to be someone else, a complete weirdo. I just…I thought we had a connection. I guess I was wrong about that too. I pulled out my phone and after some hesitation, deleted Alec's number. Now it really felt official. I wondered why I was so upset about this; it's not even like we were dating. But it was the closest I'd ever gotten to having a boyfriend and I was sad that it turned out this way. My thoughts then turned to my dad, and worry filled my body. My dad didn't look so good. He looked like a ghost of himself, pale and thin. And what was with those bruises and the constant sleepwalking? I frowned and hoped he would take my advice about seeing a doctor. My dad was really all I had. I couldn't afford for something to happen to him. I wouldn't be able to handle it. My eyes began to feel heavy and soon I was drifting off into another world...

I was unsure where I was. My surroundings were all white mist. It was cold, foggy, and silent. I walked and walked for what felt like forever. Then I saw a shape beginning to form ahead. It looked like the silhouette of a humongous castle. After a moment, I saw a figure exit the castle—a woman. She was trying to say something to me, but I couldn't hear her. I opened my mouth to speak but nothing came out. I was scared. What was happening? The woman continued trying to speak and now I could only make out a few broken words:
Help. World. Calamity.
Death.

And then I was falling into a dark abyss.

I woke up just as I was about to hit the ground. I was panting, covered in sweat. *What the hell was that?* I had never had such a vivid dream in my life. Who was that woman? She seemed so familiar but I couldn't place her. I shook my head, then looked at the clock and gasped. I'd slept for over two hours. I guess I was more tired than I thought. I thought about what Alec said, about his dreams of the world dying. Maybe his crazy ideas were making their way into my dreams.

I decided to get up and refresh myself with a shower. I took an extra long shower, allowing the warm water to hit my skin. I even sat in the shower for a moment, something I did when I was feeling particularly stressed. Eventually, I got dressed in fresh clothes and I felt a little better. Then I saw that I had five missed calls from an unknown number. I frowned and wondered who it could be. I called back the number as I was drying my hair and a woman picked up the phone.

"Thank you for calling New York Presbyterian Hospital. How can I help you?"

My heart stopped for a moment and I couldn't speak. Why would a hospital be trying to call me?

"H-hi. My name is Damien Jones and I've gotten several missed phone calls from you guys. Is there something going on?" I asked, my voice shaking.

"Just a moment," the woman told me. I held my breath. "Hi, so it looks like we've been trying to reach you because your father has been checked into the hospital."

I dropped the phone and fell to my knees, the words *your father* ringing in my head.

I picked up the phone and I asked if he's alright.

"He's in stable condition, but he passed out in front of his apartment complex. A neighbor found him and called 911."

Oh my God. "I…I'll be there as soon as I can," I said. What the hell was happening?

I ran out of the building and took a taxi to the hospital. Luckily it wasn't far. I threw money at the driver then sprinted into the hospital building. I asked the front desk woman what room Samuel Jones was in and she asked if I was family. I wanted to scream at her but I restrained myself. I told her I was his son and she gave me the room number. I raced out of the elevators and I barged into my father's room.

My heart sank when I saw him. He was lying in the hospital bed and he looked so…*frail.* He looked so pale and he was hooked up to a heart monitor. He looked up at me and smiled weakly.

"Hey, kiddo," he said casually.

"What the hell happened?" I yelled.

My dad sighed and was silent for a moment. "I went to…leave for work. And as I was about to get into my car, I felt…odd. Lightheaded and dizzy. I was going to sit down in the car when I just passed out onto the pavement. Luckily a neighbor saw and quickly called the hospital."

I shook my head and sat down. "Dad…something is wrong. You look pale and you have these strange bruises. You have migraines and are sleepwalking, and now you faint?"

I knew something was really wrong with my father. My dad was silent.

"What do the doctors think?" I asked.

He shook his head. "They've been running all sorts of tests but they can't find anything seriously wrong with me."

I was bewildered. "What do you mean? Obviously there is something wrong here!"

I thought about what Alec said before. He had mentioned my dad and said that something was wrong. But no. That was just a coincidence, right? Alec was just crazy, right? I shook my head at my own stupidity.

"I'll stay here with you," I said and sat down on the chair next to him.

"No, you should go back to school," my dad said.

"I'm staying," I said firmly.

My dad sighed. "You always were a stubborn boy."

I smiled. "Get some rest."

My dad nodded and eventually went to sleep while I sat there, lost in my thoughts. Tears glistened my eyes. What in the world was going on? Could Alec know what was wrong with my father? *That's crazy*, I told myself. How would he know anything about this when the doctors couldn't even figure it out? Could Alec really be telling the truth?

I guess there was only one way to find out.

As it got dark, I decided to finally leave the hospital. My dad reassured me that he would be fine and that he would call me with any updates. I gave him a hug and took a taxi back to the dorms. I looked at my phone to text Alec, then I remembered I deleted his number. *Dammit.* I opened my dorm room and Karina was there, unpacking. She must've seen the distraught expression on my face because she immediately asked what was wrong. I explained to her the situation and she shook her head in disbelief.

"I'm so sorry, Damien. Did the doctors have any answers?"

I shook my head. "They don't know anything."

Karina frowned. "Damn. That's so bizarre. I know your dad and he's a pretty healthy and fit guy. I wonder what it could be."

I sat on the couch and Karina sat next to me. Tears began to fall from my eyes.

"It's just...my dad is all I have. I can't afford to lose him too."

Karina hugged me. "You won't. I'm sure he will be fine. Everything will be fine."

I wanted to believe her, I did. I just wasn't so sure anymore. I sniffed and told her that I needed to contact Alec but I'd deleted his number after an argument we had. Karina was silent for a moment.

"What is it?" I asked.

Karina sighed. "Okay. So after you told me you were going on a date with Alec, I was a bit worried. I didn't want you going after some bad guy who might be trouble. So I sort of snooped around online and maaay have found out what room he's living in."

My mouth fell open, speechless.

"You really are the best," I finally said and she grinned. "So," I continued. "What's the room number?"

Luckily Alec's dorm was not too far from mine. My heart hammered in my chest and I wondered if I was doing the right thing. I walked out the elevator and went to the last room on the left hand side. I took a deep breath and tentatively knocked on the door. A moment of silence went by before the door opened, then there was Alec, eyes wide.

"Damien," he said.

I looked at his blue eyes and gathered myself. "Look, I'm still mad at you. But my dad is in trouble and I might need your help."

Alec nodded and opened the door wider for me to come in. I sighed and entered the room. It looked pretty similar to mine, but smaller. There was no one else in here so I assumed Alec didn't have a roommate. I stood in the middle of the room and I didn't know what to say at this point. I didn't think I'd get this far.

"What's happening with your dad?" Alec asked after a moment.

I kept my back toward him. "He's...he's in the hospital right now. Apparently, he passed out in the parking lot." I turned to face him. "But it's not just that... You saw how he looked at his apartment. He's pale, and looks like he hasn't slept at all. He's sleepwalking and having these intense headaches." I paused for a moment, but Alec didn't say anything. "You…you said something is wrong. And then you mentioned my dad." I narrowed my eyes. "Do you know something?"

Alec was silent. My voice rose. "If you know something, you have to tell me. My dad is in danger!" I yelled.

Alec finally looked at me and said, "I tried to tell you. And you shut me out. You didn't believe anything I told you."

I was at a loss for words. "How did you expect me to believe you? You were going on about world ending prophecies and visions and dreams!"

Alec looked down. "I know that. I know it's hard to believe. I didn't believe it at first, either. But I'm not lying, really."

I sat down on his bed. Tears glistened my eyes and I couldn't believe I was beginning to cry again. "I just want things to go back to how they were," I choked out.

Alec nodded and sat next to me. There was a moment of silence.

Alec turned to me. "I want you to know that I would never intentionally hurt you. Ever. All I want to do is help you."

I sniffed and I felt another sense of déjà vu.

"Then, please. Tell me what's happening to my dad."

Alec sighed. "Let me start from the beginning."

I nodded and waited for him to continue.

"For a long time now, I've been having dreams and vivid visions. They were at first hard to make out, but became clearer as time went on. There was a man who was warning of the world coming to an end. He told me to find some prince." Alec fidgeted with his sleeve and continued. "I…I think that the prince is you. And I think there is some sort of…malevolent entity out there who wishes you harm."

I was so confused, I didn't even know where to begin. "You're…you're saying that I'm some sort of prince?" I laughed at this. "I'm no prince. I'm just a normal college student who wants to be an actor. My dad is a mechanic. I don't have any royal blood in my body."

Alec looked at me seriously. "You said you would try and believe me."

I nodded hesitantly and said, "Okay, okay. Keep going."

Alec cleared his throat. "I kept looking for you because these dreams tell me that you're the key to stopping this evil."

I shook my head, bewildered. "Even if what you're saying is somehow true…how does my dad fit into all of this?"

Alec was quiet for a moment. "That part, I'm still unsure. But…" he trailed off.

"But what?" I asked, wanting answers.

"I have a theory," Alec said. I nodded impatiently.

"I...I think it could be..." Alec looked down and then looked me in the eye. "I think your father could be possessed."

CHAPTER 9

Present Day, New York

Damien

"Possessed? What do you mean? Possessed by what?" I looked at Alec.

He stayed quiet for a couple moments. "I'm not exactly sure. But I've been doing some research on your dad's behavior and it looks like it could be..." Alec trailed off.

"Could be what?" I pressed.

Alec sighed. "I think it could be some sort of...malevolent or even a demonic entity."

I gaped at him. "You're saying my father is possessed by a *demon*?"

Alec looked away. "It's just a theory," he muttered.

I shook my head in disbelief. "If what you're saying is even possible...how do we...*unpossess* him?"

"I'm not sure. I still need to do more research on this. Do you want to visit the library with me tomorrow after rehearsal?"

I looked at him, confused. "Why the library?"

He shrugged. "Sometimes you can find information there you can't find on Google. I figured it was worth a shot."

I sighed and nodded. "Alright. I'll go."

At rehearsal for *Carrie*, my mind was someplace else. I was trying my best to focus but it was hard when I was so worried about my dad. I kept thinking about what Alec had said. *I think your father is possessed.*

"Alright," Ms. Simmons said. "We're gonna try and block the prom scene with Damien and Alec."

Alec and I went up on stage and read our lines at the table, but my heart wasn't in it. I was thinking about our next move. After rehearsal, we'd go to the library and research how to *unpossess* my dad, as unbelievable as that sounds. I was terrified of what we might find. We then tried to block the dance scene, but I was terrible at dancing. Alec seemed to be a pretty good dancer, so I tried to follow his lead. It was the part where Carrie and Tommy have their first slow dance at prom—and also where they kiss. Shit, I forgot I was going to have to kiss Alec. Ms. Simmons didn't have us kiss today, but I knew we had to eventually.

When rehearsal finally ended and as I was about to leave with Alec to the library, Ms. Simmons stopped me.

"Damien, can I talk to you for a moment?" she asked.

Shit. She must have noticed that I didn't have my head in the game today.

"Are you doing alright?" she asked. I nodded. She continued, "I only ask because it just seemed like you weren't one hundred percent present."

I was silent for a moment. "My dad's in the hospital," I explained.

Ms. Simmons looked at me with empathy. "Damien, I'm so sorry to hear that. If you need to take time off rehearsal to be with him, I completely understand."

I shook my head immediately. I didn't want to be a detriment to the cast. "I'll be fine," I reassured her.

"Alright. As long as you're sure," she said.

I left the room to find Alec waiting for me in the hallway.

"Everything alright?" he asked and I nodded. "Let's do this."

I felt overwhelmed in the massive library.

"So what exactly are we looking for?" I asked Alec.

He walked ahead of me and said, "I'm looking for books on anything that have to do with demonology or the occult."

I still couldn't believe we were actually doing this. We walked up the stairs to find a worker to ask where books like this would be. We eventually found an older woman and she pointed us to a small section hidden in the corner—a section that looked like it didn't get many visitors. The section read OCCULT SCIENCES AND PARAPSYCHOLOGY.

I looked at Alec. "Where should we start?"

He shrugged and just started pulling random books out and flipping through them. I decided to do the same. The first book was about reincarnation and past lives. It didn't seem to have to do with demons or the occult, but I flipped through it anyways, curious. The book explained how some people in this world claimed to have memories of a past life. Someone claimed to have been a pilot in World War II, and another person claimed to have been a Hollywood agent. I found it hard to believe, but it was interesting, I'll give it that much. We looked through more books but didn't seem to find anything that resonated with us. I was about to lose hope when Alec said, "Wait."

He pulled out a dusty, leather-bound book and I leaned over to look at it. It was a grimoire on sorcery, titled *The Lesser Key of Solomon.*

"What is that?" I asked.

Alec flipped through the book and said, "I…I think it's a recording of various demons." He flipped to a page titled *The Seventy Two Demons.* There was a list of names and what appeared to be a corresponding list of sigils.

"I'm gonna check this book out," Alec said.

"Do you think that book is somehow linked?" I asked.

"I'm not sure, but my intuition is telling me that it is. And my intuition is usually right."

I got a strong sense of déjà vu, but I had been getting a lot of that lately so I brushed it off. Alec suggested we go to the reading room, so I took the book on past lives and reincarnation with me. Inside, Alec flipped through the grimoire as I flipped through the book on reincarnation. I read an excerpt:

> *Some people will go their whole lives without remembering who or what they were in the past. We think that when death greets someone, they remember all of their lives. Some people claim to also have visions or dreams of their past lives. We even believe that some people from past lives are able to reunite in their present lives.*

I thought about the dream I'd had recently, about the woman and her words of death and destruction. I thought about what Alec said, about someone looking like me and issuing a warning of calamity. *Could this really be true? Could I…have really been some sort of prince in my past?* It just didn't seem possible. None of it seemed possible. I was never one to believe in things like reincarnation or even astrology. Now…I wasn't sure about anything. I looked at Alec as he intensely studied the grimoire. I thought about my dad and how frail he was in the hospital bed. Before I knew it, my throat was clogged up and tears glistened my eyes. *Seriously, again?* I was such a crybaby.

Alec must have sensed something and looked over at me. "Hey, you alright?" he asked.

I started to nod but then shook my head. Alec put his warm hand over mine.

"It will be alright. No matter what happens, I will be there for you. I will *always* be there for you."

I smiled and nodded, tears trickling down my face. I knew he was telling me the truth and that he meant it when he said that.

I looked at him. "Thank you," I sniffed. "Did you find anything in that book?"

Alec sighed. "I never realized how many alleged demons exist. Even if the demon is one recorded in this book, I don't know how we're going to decipher which one is hurting your dad."

I was silent for a moment, trying to come up with a solution for us. "Can I see?"

Alec handed me the book. I flipped through it, trying to see if anything stood out to me. Nothing did at first, but then I frowned. There is an illustration of a young boy with angelic wings and riding what looked like a two-headed dragon. I felt like I've seen it before, somewhere.

"This image," I said and pointed to it.

Alec looked at the drawing. "Do you recognize it?" he asked.

I squinted. "I'm not sure. I feel like I might have seen it somewhere, but I can't remember anymore."

Alec took the book and studied the image. "Ualac," he read.

My stomach dropped. "What did you say?"

"That's what this demon is called. Ualac."

"That's it. That's the one," I said all of a sudden.

Alec turned to me, wide eyed. "Are you *sure*?" he asked. I nodded, although I didn't know how. "Does it say how to defeat it?" I asked.

Alec flipped through the book and shook his head.

I sighed and said, "Well, that's helpful."

"At least we might know the name of this demon." He paused for a moment. "Maybe your dad needs an exorcism."

I gaped at him. "An *exorcism*? That's the kind of stuff you...you only see in horror movies!" I shouted-whispered since we were still in the library.

Alec shrugged defensively. "It's the most obvious solution to defeating a demon, don't you think?"

I thought about it for a moment and realized I had no better solution to offer. I thought of *The Exorcist* and I shuddered. Was this really the only solution we have?

On the walk back, I thanked Alec.

Alec looked at me and said, "For what?"

"Just for...for helping me. Even though I didn't believe you at first, you still didn't hesitate to help me. I really appreciate that."

Alec nodded and said, "I told you. I'm always here for you."

I nodded and eventually we made it back to the campus. We were about to go our separate ways, but I didn't want to say goodbye just yet.

"Alec!" I called out. He stopped walking and turned around. "Do you… do you want to grab a coffee?"

Alec smiled and nodded.

We were sitting at Starbucks moments later, me with my usual pink Frappuccino and Alec with his usual dark coffee.

"I figure we could use a light break from all this…demon stuff," I said.

Alec laughed and agreed, taking a sip of his coffee. Really, I was trying to get my mind off things and talking to Alec seemed to help.

"So…you said you're from Pennsylvania right?" I asked.

Alec nodded. I asked him hesitantly if he'd lived there by himself.

Alec was silent for a moment. "No. I lived with my uncle. He took me in after my parents died."

I nodded. My heart went out to him. It felt like part of me died when my mother passed. I couldn't imagine losing both of my parents. Alec went on even though I didn't ask him to.

"The thing is…I come from a wealthy background," he said. "When my parents died, they left behind a lot of money for my uncle and me. They wanted me to have a good future in case they weren't around someday. That's why I came to this school. I'd promised that I would go to college and have a bright future, just like they wanted."

I smiled and I realized Alec really was a good person. Alec looked away.

"Actually…that's not the only reason why I came here," Alec continued. "I also came here…because I was looking for someone like you. Someone who could accept me. Something always felt like it was missing in my life, and not just my parents but…something else was lacking. I feel like I've found it, though."

I was stunned. "I…I feel the same," I finally said.

Alec smiled and he seemed happy to hear this. I had some questions though.

"I'm just curious…if you were looking for me, why did you act like you hated me in the beginning?"

Alec looked down at his coffee. "When…when I started having these dreams and visions of you, I resented them. I didn't want them. I didn't want to be someone who had to try and save the world. It made me resent you too, at first." I nodded. Alec continued, "But after I got to know you more…I realized that you were the piece that was missing. I know that sounds cheesy, but it's true."

My heart was beating fast and I felt butterflies in my stomach. "I feel the same, Alec. Thank you…for being there for me."

Alec blushed and it was so cute. We sat in a sweet silence as we sipped our drinks. Even if we didn't talk, just being together made me feel at ease. I felt like I could breathe better. Eventually, it began to get dark and Alec and I said goodbye. I felt like Alec wanted to say something else, but he just smiled and waved. I waved back and I headed to my dorm, the butterflies still fluttering in my stomach.

CHAPTER 10

Present Day, New York

Damien

That weekend, my dad was released from the hospital and he returned to his apartment. When I went to visit him, I found him standing there in his pajamas even though it was the middle of the day. He had dark circles under his eyes and looked even paler than before. I bit back my worry and stepped inside to give him a hug.

"How are you feeling?" I asked and my dad smiled weakly.

"I'm hanging in there. I just feel really tired."

I sat down on the pleather couch and Luna jumped into my lap, meowing. I scratched behind her ear absently, and I asked if the doctors were able to come up with anything. My dad just shook his head. I wondered if I should tell him about all this demon stuff, but I knew he wouldn't believe me. My dad wasn't a very superstitious man and I knew he didn't believe in demons, ghosts, aliens, or really anything of that nature.

"I'm sorry to make you worry about me," my dad said.

"Don't apologize. I am worried, but it's absolutely not your fault," I assured him.

My dad went into the kitchen to make us some tea when I heard him begin to cough violently. I ran up from the couch, Luna jumping out of my lap. I asked my dad if he was alright. He began coughing something into the sink. I gasped and almost screamed.

It was blood.

I went into the bathroom and I called Alec. A couple of rings went by as I prayed he would answer.

"Hello?" his familiar voice said.

"My dad just coughed up blood and he still looks terrible."

"It's getting worse," he finally said.

"Could you…do you think you could come over?" I asked tentatively.

"Of course. I'll start heading over now."

"Thank you, Alec," I said. I hung up the phone and went to check on my dad. He was sleeping in his room now, and I put a cold towel on his forehead. I felt angry instead of scared now. Whatever the fuck this is, I wasn't going to let it harm my dad. I would banish it back to Hell myself if I have to.

Alec arrived wearing a beanie and his striped sweater. "Thank you for coming," I said and let him in. Alec walked in and pet Luna, who lied on her back for stomach scratches.

"I've been thinking," I started. Alec looked at me and nodded for me to go on. "I'm out of options and the doctors don't know anything. My dad is getting worse, and I don't think there is much time left. I think it's time. To try the…exorcism."

Alec nodded. "I did some research and printed out a list of nearby churches and priests who may be author-ized to perform the exorcism".

I looked at the list and sighed. "Let's call some of them," I said finally.

We called a bunch of churches and nothing. Most of them didn't pick up, and the ones that did didn't want to perform the exorcism. They said it was too dangerous and deemed taboo in this day and age. I was at a loss.

"Are we able to perform the exorcism ourselves?" I asked Alec.

Alec shook his head. "I don't think it would work."

We were silent for a moment when the phone rang. Alec and I looked at each other and I picked it up.

"…Hello?" I said into the phone.

There was a moment of silence before a man's deep voice answered. "My name is Father Taylor. I…I heard you were inquiring about an exorcism?"

I looked at Alec. "Um, yes…it's my dad. His health has been declining and I think it's possible he could…be possessed. He's been sleepwalking, has random bruises, and he just started coughing up blood."

There was some silence on the other end.

"Yes…those do sound like signs of demonic posses-sion. I'm not certain I can help you at this point. It sounds like, based on your fathers' symptoms, that the possession is…almost complete."

I clutched the phone. "Please. I don't know where else to turn to at this point. I need you to at least try. Please."

More silence on the other end. Then Father Taylor said, "Alright. I will try to help you and your father. But I cannot guarantee that it will be successful. And…" he paused. I was scared for what Father Taylor was about to say next. "And…your father might not make it out alive."

I refused to believe that. I would not let my father die—not if I had anything to say about it. I gave the priest my address and he said he would try to be there as soon as possible. Alec and I sat there in silence. I began to cry and Alec embraced me. He didn't say anything and I'm grateful he didn't try to console me. He just hugged me and let me cry into his shoulder. He stroked my hair and I breathed a little slower. Whatever this evil is, I would not let it take my father.

Eventually, there was a knock at the door. I got up and I opened it. Standing there was who I assumed was Father Taylor. He was wearing a suit and had short, dark black hair and seemed like he could be in his late forties or fifties. I allowed him to enter and he closed his eyes. He didn't say anything. Then he opened his brown eyes. "Where is your father?" he asked.

I pointed to his room, and then Father Taylor looked at Alec and me. "I will first bless this house. Then I will start the exorcism. But I'm afraid I will need you two to leave while I perform the exorcism."

I immediately shook my head. "No. I'm not leaving my dad's side."

The priest narrowed his eyes. "This is a dangerous setting. You both could get seriously injured. Or worse."

I refused, but Alec stood up. "I think he may be right. We should step out while he does this."

I was flabbergasted. "No! I am not leaving—"

"Damien," Alec interrupted me. "Think about what your dad would want. He would never want you to be in danger or get hurt. Please. Trust me."

I was silent for a moment. Luna stared at me with her dark eyes. "O…Okay" I finally said and stood up. I scooped up Luna and before we left, I looked at the priest and I said, "Please. Don't hurt him."

The three of us walked out of the complex to take a walk around the neighborhood. We were silent for most of the way, but eventually Alec looked at me.

"How are you feeling?" he asked. I sighed and I held my arms around Luna.

"I'm scared. I'm scared the exorcism will fail. I'm scared of my father…" I didn't finish the sentence. There was no point. Alec knew what I meant anyway. Alec nodded and I could tell he wanted to console me, to promise me that everything would be fine. But he knew he couldn't promise that. We sat on some swings in a nearby park.

"When I was younger, I went to a park with my father and mother. I must have been around six or seven. I was swinging on the swing set, just like this one." I swung back and forth with Luna and went on. "All of a sudden, a swarm of bees attacked us. They just…came out of nowhere and seemed to focus on only my mom and me. My dad yelled to run and then he…purposefully started agitating them so they would focus on stinging him and not my mom and me." I stroked Luna's fur. "He had to go to the hospital and had about over twenty stings everywhere."

Tears fell from my eyes onto Luna's fur, and she licked herself. Alec looked at me from the other swing. "That was brave of your dad."

I nodded in agreement. "My dad was willing to put himself in danger to protect my mom and me. That's the kind of man he is. And now…" I looked away. "I need to do the same for him."

Alec looked into the distance. We sat there in silence, the three of us. After some time, we decided to go back to the apartment complex. As we walked back, I saw Father Taylor standing at the bottom of the stairs. I ran to him and I asked him what happened. The priest sighed and was silent for a moment. My stomach dropped.

"The demon that has…attached itself to your father is a strong entity. It…it's feeding off him. I tried my best to send the demon back to where it came from. It seems like I was successful for the moment and was able to suppress it, but…" he paused.

"But what?" I asked.

"It's possible that it could come back. That's how powerful it is. It lusts for power and is willing to destroy anything that gets in its way."

I took a shaky breath. "How is he?"

"He's fine for the time being. He was asleep the whole time. He won't remember any of it."

I nodded and looked down. "Thank you, Father Taylor. For trying."

He nodded and gave me a card with his phone number on it. "Give me a call if you have any updates."

I nodded and then Father Taylor left. Alec and I went back into the apartment and I put Luna down. I went into my father's room and my dad was sleeping in his bed. I kissed his forehead, and I closed the door quietly as I left.

Back at Alec's dorm, we reassessed the situation.

"Well, at least the exorcism was somewhat successful," Alec said. I knew he was doing his best to make me feel better. I nodded. I looked up and stared at Alec. Alec turned and looked back at me. This man had stuck with me through all of this shit. He could have decided to leave me in my time of need, but he didn't. He stuck with me and encouraged me to keep *going*. I stared into his clear blue eyes and the freckles that scattered across his pale face. I leaned in and I pressed my lips against his. I felt like I was exploding.

Alec tentatively kissed me back and I opened my mouth a bit wider, inviting him in. Alec pushed his tongue in, and I felt it enter my mouth. I hesitantly pushed my tongue in his mouth too and our tongues were exploring each other. I stroked his beautiful dark hair and Alec caressed my face with his hands. We pulled apart, both of us breathing heavily. Alec pressed his forehead against mine.

"Do you…?" Alec trailed off.

I smiled and nodded, our foreheads still touching. We resumed kissing and our hands were exploring each other's bodies. I took my shirt off and Alec took his shirt off too. I softly gasped; his body was beautiful. He had defined pecs and short black hairs dusted across his chest. He had defined abdominal muscles with a dark happy trail. Suddenly I felt self-conscious; I was pretty skinny and my body wasn't as defined as his. Alec seemed to know what I was thinking because he looked at me and said, "You're beautiful."

I almost swooned right then and there. I touched his chest and stroked his dark nipples and he moaned a little. I leaned in and kissed him again while playing with his nipples. After we broke apart, Alec undid my belt and unzipped my jeans. I shrugged them off, now just in my red briefs. Alec smiled when he saw what was underneath—an erect penis dripping with pre-cum. I took off

Alec's trousers and his black boxers. We were both standing there naked, our hard cocks in the air. I figured Alec would be hung, but I was not prepared for just how big he was. Alec leaned in and laid me down on his bed. He kissed me deeply and ran a hand down my torso, finally guiding himself to my cock. He gave it a couple of soft strokes and I moaned into his mouth. He asked me to lie on my stomach and I did. He ran a hand down my back to my ass.

"Your ass is amazing," he said, and I laughed. He playfully spanked it and I yelped. He kissed my ass cheeks and pressed kisses down my back. He spread my cheeks and then began lapping at my hole. I almost jumped up from how good it felt. He teased my hole with his warm tongue and pressed soft kisses to my ass. He then inserted a finger in my hole and I almost gasped at the intrusion. Alec removed his finger and then got up to grab something from the dresser. I heard a bottle uncap and he massaged my hole with his finger covered in lubricant. I heard him unwrap something as he told me to turn around. When I did, I saw him with a condom in his hand.

I nodded and I said, "I want you inside me. *Now.*"

Alec grinned and put on the condom. He spread my legs and kissed my thighs and feet.

"I...I'm gonna put it in, ok?" he asked.

I nodded. I was ready. I could feel him press his head against my wet hole and then I felt the head pop inside, and I moaned.

"Does it hurt?" Alec asked.

I shook my head and told him to keep going. He pushed in more until his full length was inside me. We stayed like this for a bit, letting it settle in.

"Can I move now?" Alec asked.

I nodded. Alec began slowly moving in and out, and *god* it felt amazing. I wrapped my legs around his back and put my hands around his neck, pulling him in closer. Alec leaned down and kissed me while he thrusted into me. I felt so loved. Alec began stroking me while he pushed in and out and it was too much. I warned Alec that I was close. Alec nodded and said he was too.

I looked at him and said, "Let's come together."

Alec continued stroking me furiously and rocking into me. A moment later, we both cried out together. Cum spurted out of my cock and flew all over me, hitting me in the face. Alec groaned and he looked so beautiful while he climaxed. Alec slumped on me and was quiet for a moment. We just stayed like this, with his softening penis still in my ass. We eventually recovered and Alec slowly pulled out of me, and I felt empty again. He looked at me, covered in cum and grinned. He trailed a finger down my stomach and licked up some of my cum. I grinned back and we kissed, cum mixing in our mouths. We pulled apart and Alec looked at me and smiled sweetly.

I love this man.

The following day was another rehearsal for *Carrie*. We were almost to the opening day. It'd been hard to focus with all this demonic stuff happening, but I'd been trying my best and had most of my lines memorized. We'd just finished practicing the scene where Tommy asks Carrie to prom, and now we are about to practice the dance scene again. Alec came over and sat at the prom table next to me while the tech crew finished setting up their equipment.

"So, how has your dad been doing?" Alec asked.

"I talked to him on the phone and he doesn't seem to remember the exorcism, just like Father Taylor said," I explained. "But he said he feels a lot better. He says he's been getting good sleep, and the sleepwalking has stopped."

Alec smiled at the news. "That's great! Maybe the exorcism really did work, after all."

"I really hope so," I said. I thought about what Father Taylor said, how he was able to suppress it, but that it could return. Anxiety filled me and I really hoped this wasn't the case. Alec could see the worry in my eyes and switched the topic.

"So…what did you think of yesterday?" Alec asked shyly. I wasn't sure what he was referring to at first but then I remembered. I blushed and looked around.

"It was…incredible," I admitted. Alec grinned at this, and I blushed even harder.

"It really was," Alec agreed.

"We'll…have to do that again sometime…if you want to."

Alec looked at me as if I were crazy. "Of course I want to!" he exclaimed. We both laughed and then it was time to start rehearsing our scene.

A long time ago
The final meeting

After that incident with my father, I decided to sneak out and see Alec once last time. I could feel my heart break. But I knew it was for the best; that our love could never be and he deserved a better future. I rode out to Dynalis with Lola and stopped behind the castle near the gardens, once again. Prince Alec was there, tending the gardens and he looked delighted to see me. I felt horrible because I knew I was about to break his heart. He must have seen the sorrow on my face.

"What's wrong?" Alec asked, concern in his eyes.

I sighed. "It's…my father. He found out about me sneaking out." I paused. "I think it's best if stopped meeting from now on." Alec looked down and was silent for a moment. He sat down on the bench and I sat next to him.

"I knew this day was coming," Alec said.

I smiled sadly. "You and I both know this is a love that can never be. You deserve better."

Alec looked at me wide-eyed and said, "I want you. That is all I want."

I could feel tears welling in my eyes and I was at a loss for words. Alec seemed lost in thought when he looked up at me.

"What if we run away together?" he said suddenly.

I had to make sure my hearing was alright. I could not believe Alec would even suggest that.

"No. We can't leave our people and you deserve better than a life on the run," I said firmly.

Alec took my hands and said, "We don't have to be on the run. I own a piece of land far east by the beaches. A beautiful cabin. We can spend our days there, playing in the water and admiring the view."

I smiled because it sounded like a dream. I wondered if it was even possible. I wanted that more than anything else in the world. I didn't want to live in that dark castle anymore with my cold-hearted father. I shook my head.

"Even if that were possible…what about our people?" I asked.

"The people of our kingdoms will still have my uncle and your father and their royal courts. They'll survive without us and still prosper."

I sat there in silence and I knew that it was a dream I could not reach. And then I surprised myself by looking up at him and saying, "Okay. I will go with you."

Alec looked delighted and kissed me. "It will be the start of a new life," he said.

I nodded and I really hoped this dream could come true. I hoped I could have this happy dream, for once in my life.

CHAPTER 11

Present Day, New York

Damien

The following day, Karina and I were sitting at our usual table at Starbucks. She wore her blond hair in her signature bun and donned a pale pink blouse with dark jeans. She sipped from her vanilla latte and asked me how my dad was doing.

I sighed. "He seems to be getting better."

I left out the part about the demons and the exorcism because, well, it was crazy. But it was true; my dad did seem to be getting better. His skin had more color and his bruises were starting to fade. There were no more instances of sleepwalking or passing out. I was feeling hopeful, but I didn't want to count my chickens before they hatched. Karina smiled at this news.

"Oh, and I'll be there tonight for your musical!" she said.

That's right; tonight was the premiere of the *Carrie* musical. I was excited about it. The cast had been practicing a lot and working hard. I thought it was going to be an amazing show; the first queer gender-bent retelling of *Carrie* was groundbreaking. I smiled and thanked Karina for coming to see the show.

She smiled and said, "I wouldn't miss it for the world!"

I felt a bit guilty; Karina had been such an amazing friend and I'd been keeping her in the dark about everything going on. Not because I didn't want to tell her, I just didn't want to burden her with all of this demonic shit. I was silent for a moment, but I've always been bad at hiding my emotions.

Karina sat her latte down and said, "You're not telling me something, huh?"

I quickly looked up and I opened my mouth to say no, but I couldn't lie to her.

"Is it something you can't tell me?" she asked.

I was silent and Karina nodded, but she didn't look upset.

"I understand."

I looked at her, surprised. "You do?"

She nodded. "There are things we can't tell each other sometimes, for whatever reason. Everyone hides something. And I know you'll tell me when the time is right."

I smiled and I said, "You really are the best person in the world."

Karina smiled back and said, "Yeah, I know".

Later, I called my dad to tell him he didn't have to come see the musical since he was still recovering.

"Nonsense!" my father said. "I wouldn't miss this for anything!"

I smiled to myself, then sighed and said, "Ok, obviously I can't convince you not to come. It starts at seven."

We talked for a bit more and then we hung up. I felt hopeful; my dad seemed to be doing better and I was excited for the musical. I looked at the time and it was almost five. I needed to start heading to the theater. I gathered up my backpack and was on my way.

I looked at myself in the mirror backstage. I was wearing a pure white tuxedo, a gold crown, and a sash that said PROM KING. In the beginning stages, Ms. Simmons and I had discussed how exactly we go about the musical. I had initially told Ms. Simmons I wanted it to be a gender-bent adaptation and she said that was fine. We had also considered changing Carrie's name to a more masculine name but decided to keep it in the end. The tricky thing was that we haven't actually practiced the scene where the bucket of pig's blood falls on me. Ms. Simmons wanted to save it for the actual show. The blood was made of a mixture of syrup and red food dye, just like in the original film.

I was nervous, but I was also excited. Alec walked backstage in a black tuxedo; he looked dashing. He smiled and walked over to me and squeezed my hand.

"How do you feel?" he asked and I smiled back.

"My heart is beating really fast," I admitted.

He cupped my face with his hands. "You're gonna do amazing."

Then he kissed me. I still couldn't believe this man was mine. It felt like a dream, and that whole demon fiasco felt like a nightmare I had a long time ago. Now, it was almost time for our show. I peeked out the curtains and *wow*. It was a full house out there. I saw my dad sitting near the front row. I smiled to myself, grateful to have such a good supporter. Alec helped me with my stage makeup and I helped him with his. I changed out of my suit into the costume I wore for the very first scene. Eventually, Ms. Simmons entered backstage and let us know it was time for us to get in our places. My stomach flipped and I told myself that I could do this. The curtain started rising. I took a deep breath and the lights came on and I stepped on stage, ready for the opening scene.

We eventually made it to intermission and the show was going smoothly so far. The audience seemed to be enthralled and it felt so good to be on stage again. I was backstage and reapplying some makeup when Alec came over.

"You're doing amazing," he said and I smiled.

"So are you," I said.

"Are you ready for the dance scene?"

I nodded. "I'm happy I get to dance with you."

Alec grinned his goofy grin and I almost melted to the ground.

"One minute, everyone! Back to your places!" Ms. Simmons shouted at us. I quickly changed into my white tuxedo and Alec changed into his black suit. We stepped on stage together, then sat at a round table at the prom. We went through our lines when Alec, as Tommy, asked if I wanted to dance. I smiled shyly and said not yet, just like Carrie does. There was some more prodding from Alec and we voted ourselves as the winners on the voting sheet. The familiar notes of our song started to play, so Alec and I finally got up to dance. I acted like I didn't know what I was doing and Alec put his hands on my waist and guided my hands around his neck. We danced like this for a bit and I listened to the melody of the song.

Alec leaned down and kissed me and I felt like I was in a dream. I felt like this was something I'd done before, a long time ago in the past. It felt like magic. I clutched onto Alec and closed my eyes as the finishing notes of the song played. We sat back down and the actor playing the school principal got on stage to announce the winners.

"Please welcome your Prom King…" he paused for dramatic effect. "Tommy Ross!"

Alec stood up, receiving a crown and sash. He smiled toward the audience and everyone clapped. The principal looked at the ballot.

"It looks like our next winner is…Carrie White!"

I looked up, pretending to be stunned and my eyes began to water. I went up and the prom court placed a beautiful gold crown on my head and gave me the same sash and flowers. I smiled at Alec and we held hands. This moment was one I would never forget. I was so happy, I almost forgot that the bucket of blood was about to fall onto me. After a dramatic pause and in the midst of all the clapping, the string connected to the bucket was pulled and I was doused in "pigs blood."

And then the world exploded.

CHAPTER 12

Present Day, New York

Damien

I heard screaming and at first I thought it was part of the musical. Then I heard what sounded like a bomb exploding and I realized something was wrong. I looked around the auditorium, trying to understand what was happening when I noticed something. *My father's chair was empty.* I gasped and all I tasted was syrup and sugar and I could feel the fake blood dripping down my face and body. I looked up at Alec and he had a frightened expression, but he wasn't acting anymore. He knew something was wrong too. There was another explosion and everyone began standing up and screaming, running for the exits. Now I really felt like I was in *Carrie*. I turned to Alec and tugged on his sleeve.

"It's my dad. He's not here anymore!"

Alec's eyes widened and we both knew what was happening now. We ran down the stage and outside, but I couldn't see anything. There was smoke everywhere and it felt *hot*. I felt like I've lived through this before. Through the smoke, I saw the entire surrounding area was on fire. The streets were caving in and there were bodies on the ground. I swallowed. Then I remembered Karina was here somewhere, but I couldn't see her anywhere amongst the smoke and flames.

I turned to Alec and yelled, "We have to find Karina, she's here somewhere!"

"Damien, you need to calm down!" Alec exclaimed.

I was crying and screaming and talking nonsense when I felt Alec slap me across the face. I was stunned, but it somehow helped me collect myself.

"I'm sorry," Alec said. "But I need you to focus. You are the *only* one who can stop this. I grunted angrily and looked up at him.

"I can't stop this," I cried out. "I don't have any powers. I'm nobody special. I'm not a prince or a king. I'm *nobody*!" I shouted.

Alec shook his head and put his hands on my shoulders. He looked me in the eye.

"You are not nobody. You are Damien Jones and you are the most kindhearted and loving person I know. You are worth something and I believe in you. If you can't believe in yourself, then let me do it for you!"

And then he kissed me on the face. I felt empowered. I felt like maybe I *could* stop this destruction. I nodded and took deep breaths.

"Alright. You go find Karina and get somewhere safe and I'll go look for my dad." Alec nodded and ran the opposite direction.

I ran into the streets and I yelled, "Dad! Where are you!?" and I kept shouting and screaming, trying to avoid the holes in the streets and the flames. My heart raced and I prayed that my father was alright.

Then I felt a chill run down my spine and I stopped running.

It had found me.

Alec

I was running around desperately, trying to guide people away from the fires and explosions, but most people were hysterical and wouldn't listen to me. As I was running, I saw a blond girl hiding behind some rubble. I ran to her.

"Are you alright?"

She nodded shakily.

"You're Karina, aren't you?"

She nodded and I extended my hand.

"Come on, you'll be safe with me."

Karina hesitated, then took my hand and we ran blindly together searching for a place to hide. I was praying that Damien was alright, wherever he was. Karina and I ducked into an empty classroom.

"What's happening!?"

I sighed, unsure of how to summarize the situation. "Long story short, Damien's father has been possessed by a demon and is now trying to destroy the world."

Karina shook her head in disbelief. "No wonder Damien was keeping secrets from me."

I nodded and I told her to believe in Damien. "He'll set things right," I promised.

Karina looked at me in awe. "Do you really believe in him that much?"

I nodded. "I do."

Karina slowly nodded and said, "I guess he was right. You're not so bad after all."

I smiled at this. *Oh, Damien. Please, wherever you are, I am sending you my strength.*

Damien

I slowly turned around and I almost fainted. Standing before me was my father, only it wasn't really my father. It *looked* like my father, but his kind green eyes were now a dark red and he had blue and purple veins trailing all over his face and body.

He... It...grinned at me. But it wasn't a kind grin at all. Its teeth were sharp and blood pooled in its mouth. I narrowed my eyes and collected myself, telling myself to be brave.

"Leave. My. Father. Alone. You. Fucker." I spat out.

It tilted its head and kept grinning. "So..." it said, but it wasn't my father's voice.

This voice sounded deep and monstrous and something unholy. "You are the one who sealed me long ago, the former prince of Krusada," it finished, and I frowned. *What the hell was it talking about?*

It kept looking at me and said, "I've waited so long for this moment—to extract my revenge on the prince and to possess my former host."

I shook my head. I couldn't follow what it was saying.

"What are you talking about?" I asked.

It continued smiling and slowly said, "You don't remember, hmm? Then let me show you. Our past history together, you and I who are intertwined by the fates of this world."

Then it lunged at me.

When my eyes opened, I was in some sort of ancient looking room. There were books lined along the wall and stone floors. There were stairs leading up to a door, which swung open. A tall man walked in. He was wearing long black robes and had his hood up. He lowered his hood and I gasped. It's…my father? I waited for him to see me, but it seemed like he couldn't. He pulled a book from the shelf and flipped through its pages. My eyes widened when I saw the book. It was the same one Alec found at the library. The grimoire of spells and demons, The Lesser Key of Solomon.

He began to light a bunch of candles and then started the fireplace. He drew a pentagram on the floor and began speaking a language I'd never heard before. After some strange chanting, he cut his wrist and allowed it to drip down into the fire. The fire grew, like it had been waiting for this. I could almost make out a face in the fire and my father smiled, but it was a sinister smile. He had summoned something—something that wasn't supposed to be in this world.

And then I was transported into another memory.

I saw flashes and glimpses of Alec and I. Alec and I meeting in a beautiful garden. Alec pointing his sword at me and then smiling. Alec and I dancing in a beautiful ballroom. Alec and I in a boat on a lake. Alec and I kissing under the moonlight on a balcony. Alec and I having sex.

Alec…being burned alive.

And then there was me being burned alive.

And then darkness.

CHAPTER 13

Present Day, New York

Damien

Suddenly I was back in the ruined streets of New York City and this monstrous being was standing opposite me. It tilted his head and waited. Memories were a tricky thing. Once I got one back, a whole bunch of other memories flooded my brain. Tears fell from my eyes. I understood now. My former father of my past life had summoned an unholy entity that didn't belong in this world—and now it was up to me to stop it.

I looked into its red eyes and I said, "Ualac."

It looked a bit stunned at the fact I knew its name and then collected itself and grinned again. "So… you do remember me."

I nodded. "Yes, I do. And I also remember that you don't belong in this world."

It laughed at this, a disgusting laugh. "I was born from the same sea as you; I am your kin and yet you say I don't belong here?"

I was confused by this statement, but I decided it was time to end this. "What do you want?"

I asked. It looked at me intensely and hungrily. "I want to make a new world, a world worthy that I alone can rule. And also…I want to see you *suffer*."

Then it raised its hand and black smoke blasted from it and slammed me into a tree, knocking the breath out of me.

Alec

"Something is wrong," I said.

Karina looked at me. "What do you mean?"

I shook my head and said, "I'm not sure. But I feel it. Damien is in danger."

I looked at Karina and said, "You stay here and hide. I will go to him."

Karina was about protest and then saw there was no persuading me otherwise.

She nodded. "Be safe."

"I'll try."

Damien

I woke up in a white void. I slowly got up and looked around. Nothing. Was I dead? Then I heard footsteps. I turned around and saw a figure emerge from the void. He came closer and I gasped because it was me. It was me wearing a beautiful white cloak and instead of my brown eyes, they were gold. He smiled at me and bowed. I stood there awkwardly not knowing what was happening. He stood up and unsheathed a beautiful gold sword with intricate carvings on the handle. He offered it to me.

"Why are you giving me this?" I asked.

The prince looked up at me with his golden eyes and said, "This is the only way to restore peace to this world."

Suddenly I understood and I shook my head and pushed the sword away.

"I can't. I would never hurt my father."

The prince sighed and said, "He isn't your father anymore. This is the only way."

Tears trickled my cheeks and I closed my eyes. Was he right? Was this really the only way? I hesitated.

And then I grabbed the sword.

I stood up and I must have looked like a madman. I was wearing a white suit and I was covered in what looked like blood. I felt myself clutching something and I looked down; I was holding a sword. I looked up and there was Ualac standing before me, and it was grinning.

"Do you wish to fight?" it teased.

I didn't say anything and I tightened my grip on the heavy sword. Ualac then lifted its hand and materialized a sword of its own, this one made of black metal with a red handle.

"Let us fight," it said.

It lunged toward me with its sword. I closed my eyes and I lifted up my sword, and some sort of invisible shield protected me. Ualac was thrown backwards and landed on its back. I breathed heavily. My veins were hot and I could feel a power surging through me. I felt my consciousness begin to fade and something else was taking over my body. I felt a painful sensation on my back and then my eyes turned gold.

Alec

I ran and ran, screaming Damien's name but I couldn't find him anywhere. I tried avoiding the flames and bodies as I ran wildly. Until finally I saw him standing by a tree, holding a…sword? What looked like his father was on the ground before him. The figure slowly rose, also holding a sword. I ran to Damien and shouted his name.

It wasn't Damien who looked back at me. He was covered in what looked like blood and his beautiful brown eyes were a glittering gold. He looked beautiful and monstrous at the same time. I kept running and suddenly he pointed the sword at me and I was thrown backwards. I landed hard on my back and I slowly got back up, stunned. *Did Damien just attack me?* I looked at him and he suddenly unfolded beautiful, angelic feathery wings from his back. He rose to the sky with the sword.

I saw Damien's father rise up and he too sprouted a pair of wings—only these are black and bat-like. I shook my head and wondered if I was hallucinating. As I watched this battle brew in the sky, I couldn't recognize Damien anymore. He lifted his sword.

"I am Prince Damien of Krusada. You, unholy being have trespassed onto this earth and I shall be the one to eliminate you," he proclaimed.

The malevolent being snarled and lunged toward Damien. A sword fight began. Damien dodged his father's attack while thrusting his sword at him, aiming for his head. His father blocked the attack with his sword and blew Damien back. Damien recovered and began lunging towards Ualac, anger in his golden eyes. I felt helpless as I watched.

Please, Damien. Remember the people who love you.

CHAPTER 14

Present Day, New York

Damien

"I am Prince Damien of Krusada and I shall be the one to eliminate you," I heard myself say. It was like I was watching the scene unfold from outside my body. We battled in the night sky. Ualac snarled and viciously lunged, repeatedly slashing its sword at me. I tried my best to defend myself and block its attacks, but it was relentless. We went on like this, getting nowhere it seemed. Suddenly I heard someone call my name.

"Damieeeen!" Alec shouted.

Ualac, distracted for a moment, looked down. This was my chance to finally kill this evil.

I quickly lifted up my sword and was about to strike down when I froze. Ualac had turned back to me, its eyes turned green for a split second.

"Damien," said my father's voice, kind and gentle. "Help me."

I paused for a moment, and suddenly I could feel my consciousness return. I felt my eyes turn back to brown, and I took back control of my body. I looked at the sword in my hand and I dropped it. It hit the ground with a metallic clang. I looked back up and saw Ualac grinning again, its eyes back to red.

"You've given up?" it laughed. "Someone weak like you cannot protect this world. You cannot save this world with such a pathetic light."

I breathed in and I saw Alec looking up at me. I gave him a nod, letting him know that I was ready to do the right thing. I turned back to Ualac.

"I haven't given up yet. You see, I love this world. It may be filled with grief and suffering and evil, but I still love it. Because this is the place where I got to meet all of my loved ones." I smiled warmly. "I can feel your pain and suffering and I understand your loneliness, I do."

This seemed to anger Ualac greatly and it shouted, "You understand nothing!" It blasted me with a wave of black energy. I screamed in pain but I didn't give up, not yet.

"I understand now what you want. And I will be the one to give it to you. I will embrace you and I shall save this world."

And then I flew toward Ualac with my arms spread open.

It pointed its sword at me. "Stay back!"

I dodged the sword and I embraced my father.

And then there was an explosion of light.

Then darkness.

Alec

I looked at Damien and he nodded at me. I nodded back, understanding. I smiled to myself; only Damien was capable of sympathizing with a demon. And then Damien lunged toward Ualac, embracing it. An explosion of bright white light filled the air, throwing me backwards.

When I came to, the fires were dissipating. The smoke was disappearing and the bodies on the ground were coming back to life. The sky cleared and the full moon shone brightly. I slowly stood up and looked around; ahead of me I saw Mr. Jones crumpled on the floor, unconscious. I ran to him. I felt his pulse and sighed in relief. Then I looked around for Damien, but I didn't see him anywhere. I screamed and shouted for him but…nothing. And then I saw something glittering on the floor. I slowly walked toward it and picked up the object.

It was a seahorse pendant.

Tears filled my eyes and I clutched the pendant in my hand.

"…Damien," I cried out.

EPILOGUE

...

...

...

Silence. I gained consciousness but was unable to open my eyes. I wiggled my fingers and then my toes. I finally opened my eyes and saw…nothing but white. There was no one here but me. I tried to remember what happened before, but my head was foggy. And then I heard a noise. It sounded like footsteps.

I looked up and saw a woman. Not just a woman, but a beautiful woman. She was wearing a pure white dress and she smiled warmly at me. She extended her hand to me and I took it. She helped me up and kept holding my hand.

"Walk with me," she said. She didn't say anything as we walked but I got a strong sense of déjà vu. I had a question, but I was scared of the answer. I opened my mouth, but before I could get the words out the woman finally spoke.

"Is it coming back to you?" she asked. "Do you remember what happened?"

I thought about what happened. And then it started to come back to me in waves.

"I…I tried to embrace Ualac. Even though it was a malevolent being, I could still feel its pain and loneliness. It was strange. But I understood how it felt." I wondered if I was making sense but the woman was nodding as though it did. "I tried to embrace its pain and sadness but I was thrown back at the last second." We kept walking, hand in hand. "Am I…am I dead?" I finally asked.

The woman stopped walking and released my hand as she turned to me. She smiled warmly again. "Your empathy and kindness brought about a miracle of hope that saved this world. I cannot express how proud of you I am, my beautiful son."

She stroked my cheek and suddenly it made sense. This woman was my mother from my past life! Tears glistened in my eyes and I looked at her.

"What happened to Ualac? Was I able to seal it away?" I asked.

My mother looked away. "Thanks to your show of courage and kindness, Ualac was sealed and has melted away into the Sea of Life, the place where all celestial beings come from. It may be reborn again one day, but there is no way of knowing for sure."

I looked away. "Then…this could happen all over again?" I asked.

My mother smiled and said, "Don't worry. Believe in this world and its people. Believe in yourself. If you keep that star shining bright within you, there is nothing you cannot face."

I was confused by this statement, but I nodded anyway.

"Will I ever see Alec or my father again?" I asked.

My mother was quiet for a moment and I feared what she was about to say.

"As long as there are people on Earth who remember and love you, you may return to the world of the living."

And I began to cry at this. My mother and I embraced and then I heard another pair of footsteps. I turned around and I saw…me. I was wearing a silk white cloak and a white suit. The Prince of Krusada. Prince Damien. He walked toward me and smiled.

"Thank you," he said. "Because of your courage and strength, you have freed me from the chains of this earth. We can now move on. You are no longer burdened by your past life."

I smiled and nodded, tears streaming down my face. And then the prince began to turn transparent, before fading away completely. I turned to my mother.

She smiled. "Go."

I nodded and began to run. I stopped and turned around. My mother was beginning to fade as well. "Thank you…mother".

And I ran. And ran. And ran. Until a bright white light encased me completely.

Alec

I'm not sure why I was in Central Park. It was like my body just walked here on its own without my brain's permission. I was sitting on a wooden bench, staring ahead at a beautiful lake. Ducks swam in the lake under the clear blue sky.

I was lying before; I knew why I came here. This was where Damien and I had our first date. I hadn't accepted the fact that he was gone, that he sacrificed himself to save this undeserving world. This world didn't deserve a beautiful soul like Damien. Damien, and his beautiful brown eyes and tan skin. His idealism and inability to see the worst in others. His kindness and empathy, even for those who hurt him.

Those were all traits that I didn't possess. And that is why I loved Damien. If only I had been able to tell him that. I was a fool to hide my true feelings, not realizing how life can take away love so quickly and so cruelly. I sighed and looked at the crystal clear water. I closed my eyes and listened to the ducks quack and the trees rustle in the wind. I listened to the cars on the streets and other people talking. I sat like this for a moment, appreciating but also hating the fact that I was alive and could experience these things. It wasn't worth it, not if I couldn't be with the one I love. I slowly got up and began to walk toward my dorm, lost in my own thoughts and sorrow.

"*Aaaaaaleeeec!*"

My heart stopped. Was I imagining things? I could've sworn I heard his voice. It was faint, but definitely there. Was I so lost in my grief that I was now imagining his voice in my head? I shook my head and continued walking.

And then I heard it again, louder.

"*AAAAALEEEEC!*"

I gasped and turned around. There he was.

He was running toward me and I wondered if I was hallucinating. I cried out and ran toward him too. I reached my hands out and I ran faster than I have ever ran before. The ducks were so startled that a bunch of them flew away, but I didn't care.

After what felt like forever, Damien and I finally reached each other and I embraced him tightly and I didn't let go. I would never let him go again. Tears fell from my eyes and I was lost for words.

Damien looked up at me, his eyes wet. He smiled.

"You found me."

I shook my head and said, "No, *you* found *me.*"

I didn't know how this was possible, and I didn't care. All that mattered is that he came back to me. This beautiful, kind soul. I pulled something from my pocket and gave it to Damien. Damien took it and smiled. It was his seahorse necklace.

"Thank you," he said.

I leaned down and I kissed Damien, the sun setting behind us.

Damien, you are my prince charming, in this life and the next.

THE END.

DEBAUCHERY IN THE LIBRARY

A *Princes* Short Story

A long time ago...

All I could see was pure darkness.

There was a blindfold around my eyes, and I followed the warm hand leading me around the castle. I giggled in anticipation.

"Where are we going?" I asked, even though I knew he wouldn't tell me.

"We're almost there," Prince Alec promised.

I sighed in feigned annoyance and kept walking. The truth was, I'd have followed this man anywhere blindly. It didn't matter where he'd take me. I only cared if we were there together.

Suddenly, we came to a stop. "Okay, you can take the blindfold off," Alec said. I untied the cloth, and I saw...a door.

I looked at him in confusion, raising an eyebrow. Alec laughed at my response. "You can open it," he said with amusement.

A smile tugged at my lips and I opened the door slowly. I stepped inside and gasped with amazement. The room was humongous, and beautiful, golden paper covered the walls. I twirled around, taking it all in. Statues of winged birds lined the large windows and a grand spiral staircase.

But what really made me gasp were the *books*. Books everywhere. Endless rows of shelves that reached towards the ceiling, all containing more books. I turned to Alec, who was grinning from ear to ear. I just shook my head, unable to say anything.

"There has to be at least a million books in here!" I finally shouted, my voice echoing.

Alec laughed and stepped closer. "I had a feeling you would like this room," he said, obviously pleased by my reaction.

I stepped toward one of the shelves and ran my hand along the spines of the books. "I have a library at home, but it's nothing like this," I confessed. "If I had a room like this, I would never leave."

Prince Alec kept smiling, his eyes glittering. "Then it is yours," he said casually.

I looked at him in disbelief and began to shake my head. "No one uses this room anymore," Alec explained. "My uncle received most of these books as gifts and offerings, but in truth, he is not a big reader."

He stepped closer, closing the space between us. "If you ever feel sad or lonely, you can come here. You can escape reality with any book you choose," he said, stroking my cheek.

I closed my eyes and felt hypnotized by his touch. Tears threatened to fall, and I felt a lump in my throat. I opened my eyes and stared into Alec's dazzling blue eyes. "Thank you," I whispered.

Alec pressed his forehead against mine, and I could feel his warm breath. "You don't have to be alone," he whispered back, and began nibbling on my ear. I moaned quietly and felt my heartbeat quicken.

Alec pulled back and our eyes met. He smiled gently and leaned in, pressing his lips to mine. The kiss was sweet at first, with just our lips touching. Then I could feel Alec's tongue pushing into my mouth, and I opened wider, inviting him in. I explored his mouth with my own tongue, my hand grasping at the sleeve of his robe. His tongue was warm and wet, and I could feel the blood already rushing to my groin.

Alec pulled back with a hungry expression in his eyes, and I knew he wanted more of me. I wasn't great at taking initiative during sex, but I wanted Alec so badly. It was like I wasn't in control of my own body anymore, simply watching from the outside.

I slowly fell to my knees and looked up at Alec, blinking innocently. He stared back, not smiling anymore.

"When you look at me like that, it makes me want to fuck you until there's nothing left," he said gruffly.

My cock twitched, and I slowly lowered his trousers, entranced by the large cock underneath. It was fucking *beautiful* and made my mouth water in anticipation. I'd seen Alec's cock before, but it still surprised me at how *big* and thick he was. A pair of large, meaty balls hung underneath, and I grasped them in my hand, feeling them.

"Suck on them," Alec commanded. I nodded obediently and lowered my mouth to his ballsack, licking and swirling them around in my mouth. *Fuck*, his balls were so large, it was hard to get both in my mouth. I grasped at his cock with my other hand, stroking it softly. I could hear Alec breathing heavily, trying to maintain control. I kissed and sucked his sack as I moved my hand up and down on his warm shaft.

Suddenly, I felt Alec's large hand on my head, directing my mouth to his manhood. I got the message, and I let him guide my mouth onto his cock. I teased and suckled on the mushroom-shaped head, digging my tongue into the slit at the top. I could taste his salty precum, and *fuck*, I wanted more of it.

I kept playing with his balls with one hand while I pleasured him with my mouth. I moved my lips up and down his giant cock, going deeper with each movement. "That's it. Open that throat," Alec slurred, stroking my hair.

Encouraged by this, I went deeper until my face was pressed against his dark pubic hair, and I could feel his penis enter my throat.

"Oh, fuck!" Alec shouted, and he held my head there for a few moments before slowly moving in and out, fucking my throat. I tried my best not to gag, relaxing my throat as he face-fucked me.

"Fuuuck," Alec groaned. "Can't wait to fuck your little hole, just like how I'm fucking your throat," he said, his voice low and gravelly.

After a few moments, Alec slowly pulled out, and I came up with a gasp. I breathed in and out heavily, trying to regain my composure. I looked up at Alec and he tilted his head, face expressionless. "Can't handle this big cock?" he asked, seeming almost disappointed.

I quickly shook my head and grasped at his muscular thigh. "I c-can handle your big cock," I stuttered, still breathing hard.

Alec smirked and slapped his meat against my face a couple of times. "I need you to strip," he said casually. I nodded fast and undid the clasp to my robes, letting them fall. I stepped out of my trousers and undergarments until I was completely naked.

Alec nodded approvingly. "Beautiful," he remarked, running a hand down my back to my plump ass. He slapped a cheek and playfully squeezed it, admiring it.

Alec directed me to one of the pillars lining the staircase and instructed me to bend over. I did as I was told, my heart drumming in anticipation. I could hear Alec undress, and he walked over, admiring my ass on display.

"Look at you," he said, laughing. "You look like my own personal little sex doll."

My cock thickened at this observation, and I nodded, agreeing with him. I could feel Alec slapping his cock on my ass a couple times, rubbing it in the crease of my crack. "I hope you're ready to take this cock," he said.

"I'm ready," I promised. *So fucking ready.*

Alec bent down and spread my ass cheeks, spitting into my hole. He rubbed a thumb over it, and I could feel his tongue between my cheeks, sucking at my pink hole. I jumped from how good it felt and let out a little squeal. Alec kept licking and lapping at my small hole, clutching at my ass cheeks.

He pulled back and spat into my hole again. "Can't wait to stretch this tight hole out," he said, more to himself than to me. Alec stood up, and I knew it was coming at any moment. I could feel the blunt tip of his cock begin to enter me, and I hissed at the initial burn. His hands gripped my slender hips, and he pushed in more until I was certain I would split in half.

"Oh, fuuuuck!" I shouted, unable to contain myself.

I heard Alec snicker at this. He leaned in to whisper in my ear, "I'm all in, baby." I shivered at this, and Alec pulled out halfway before slamming back in, and I yelled in both pain and pleasure. Alec gripped my hair, pushing in and out, fucking me like a madman. I knew he was in a state of mind where it didn't matter if I broke or fell apart.

He would keep fucking me. Only me. *And this turned me the fuck on.*

I felt Alec slap my ass hard as he thrusted into me. "Whose ass is this?" he asked harshly.

I was about to speak when I felt another slap. "Y-yours! Only yours!" I shouted, my voice bouncing off the walls.

Alec pulled and twisted at my brown curls as he kept rocking into me, going faster with each thrust.

"Oh, fuck, I'm close," Alec warned. I nodded fierce-ly, and pushed my ass back on his cock, inviting him to keep going. "Give me your cum!" I yelled, desperate for it, *needing* it.

"Gonna fucking fill you with my seed," Alec mum-bled, and then I could feel him ejaculate into me, filling me up. "Oh, fuuuuuck," Alec moaned, riding out his orgasm, slowing his thrusts. I could still feel him pumping ropes of his seed into me, and I felt like I was going to explode with pleasure.

Alec breathed in and out heavily, resting his head on my back, sweat dripping down his forehead. I just stood there, bent over, his cock still in my ass.

Although I didn't want him to, I could feel Alec begin to pull out, and I moaned at the sudden emptiness. I could feel his cum gush out of my ass, dripping down onto the floor.

Alec laughed to himself and inspected my well-fucked hole. "I definitely stretched you out," he said, running a thumb over my dripping hole. He licked up some of his own seed from his finger and told me to turn around. I did, and he leaned in to kiss me, and I could taste his salty cum, mixing into my mouth.

He pulled back and rested his forehead against mine. "You okay?" he whispered, back to his caring, normal self. I nodded and smiled, wrapping my arms around him.

"That was amazing," I confessed.

Alec looked away shyly. "I know you said before that you liked my…dominant nature. But are you sure it wasn't too much? Was I too rough?" he asked, his brow furrowing.

I laughed and shook my head. "I love how rough you handle me," I assured him.

Alec nodded, a smile at the corner of his mouth. "If it's ever too much, just say the word, and I'll stop," he promised. I nodded along and kept embracing Alec, never wanting to let him go. Never wanting to let this *moment* go.

"I love you," I said suddenly, unable to keep it in any longer.

Alec looked at me in surprise. "You don't have to say it back," I said quickly, unable to read his expression.

Alec laughed softly. "Actually, I wanted to say it first," he replied. A blush rose up my neck, and I laughed along with him. We just stood there, embracing, naked and laughing together. *So, this is what love feels like*, I thought to myself.

I only hoped I could hold onto them.

That feeling of love, and this man.

Acknowledgments

As a gay man, I'm always looking for queer romance tales. Luckily, there have been more and more lately but still the romance section is heavily dominated by M/F romance. Having said that, this is a story I would have absolutely loved to have read as a teenager!

I've always wanted to write a book and there are many people who I must thank for making this dream possible.

Thank you to my mom and dad who always supported my dreams and encouraged me to never give up. Writing this story would not have been possible without your love and support. I love you both dearly!

Thank you to my brother and sister for always being there for me! You both also encourage and lift me up. I know you both got my back, and I've always got yours.

A huge thank you to my editor, Thea! You did a phenomenal job, and this book wouldn't have been possible without your hard work!

Thank you to May for the amazing cover art. I loved seeing Damien and Alec being brought to life and you did an awesome job!

Thank you to Paul for the beautiful formatting of this book! I really appreciate all of your work!

Thank you to my best friend, Kai, for always being there for me and believing in me. You've always had faith in me from the beginning and I really appreciate that. I hope you enjoy this story!

Thank you to my cousins Sidra and Sabrina for also encouraging me to write! I started writing this story the day after you told me to just write, and so this story might not exist without your encouragement!

Thank you to Angel Payne for all of your advice and help! I felt a bit lost during the publishing process and your guidance really helped me.

And finally, thank YOU for giving this story a chance! I really hope you enjoy this story and that it resonates with you in some way. Thank you for joining Damien and Alec on their journey! And who knows? This might not be the end of their story…;)

About the Author

Noah Khan was born in Los Angeles and raised in Orange, California. Just like Damien, he dreams of becoming an actor. He writes songs and records music as a hobby and released his first EP on Spotify. He's also an avid collector of dolls and stuffed animals and is a huge queer romance reader. He *might* have also been a prince in his past life. He has three pets: two dogs and a parrot. *Princes* is his first published work.